"Are you going to be my lifelong bodyguard?"

Chace turned Ellie to face him. Now that she brought up the idea, he wasn't sure he'd mind keeping an eye on her. It was crazy, but he couldn't deny it. It didn't mean he wanted to make any kind of commitment or declare his undying love, but the thought of being with her felt...right.

"For this trip, I'm responsible for you."

In the dim light, he couldn't see her face clearly. The silence surrounded them, and he could have sworn he heard her heart beating. Or was that his own, racing in his ears? He pressed her hand to his chest and drew her close.

"Chace," she said on a whispered breath.

It was then he knew who he should be protecting her from.

Dear Reader,

I hope the long hot summer puts you in the mood for romance—Silhouette Romance, that is! Because we've got a month chock-full of exciting stories. And be sure to check out just how Silhouette can make you a star!

Elizabeth Harbison returns with her CINDERELLA BRIDES miniseries. In *His Secret Heir,* an English earl discovers the American student he'd once known had left with more than his heart.... And Teresa Southwick's *Crazy for Lovin' You* begins a new series set in DESTINY, TEXAS. Filled with emotion, romance and a touch of intrigue, these stories are sure to captivate you!

Cara Colter's THE WEDDING LEGACY begins with *Husband by Inheritance.* An heiress gains a new home—complete with the perfect husband. Only, he doesn't know it yet! And Patricia Thayer's THE TEXAS BROTHERHOOD comes to a triumphant conclusion when *Travis Comes Home.*

Lively, high-spirited Julianna Morris shows a woman's determination to become a mother with *Tick Tock Goes the Baby Clock* and Roxann Delaney gives us *A Saddle Made for Two.*

We've also got a special treat in store for you! Next month, look for Marie Ferrarella's *The Inheritance*, a spin-off from the MAITLAND MATERNITY series. This title is specially packaged with the introduction to the new Harlequin continuity series, TRUEBLOOD, TEXAS. But *The Inheritance* then leads back into Silhouette Romance, so be sure to catch the opening act.

Happy Reading!

Mary-Theresa Hussey

Mary-Theresa Hussey
Senior Editor

Please address questions and book requests to:
Silhouette Reader Service
U.S.: 3010 Walden Ave., P.O. Box 1325, Buffalo, NY 14269
Canadian: P.O. Box 609, Fort Erie, Ont. L2A 5X3

A Saddle
Made for Two

Roxann Delaney

SILHOUETTE *Romance*

Published by Silhouette Books

America's Publisher of Contemporary Romance

To Cindy and Tracy, my favorite mother-and-daughter
barrel racers, for always being there to answer my
questions. To the wonderful ladies and gents
of Cata-romance, the very best group in cyberspace.
And to my mom, for always believing in me.

 SILHOUETTE BOOKS

ISBN 0-373-19533-8

A SADDLE MADE FOR TWO

Copyright © 2001 by Roxann Farmer

Visit Silhouette at www.eHarlequin.com

Printed in U.S.A.

Books by Roxann Delaney

Silhouette Romance

Rachel's Rescuer #1509
A Saddle Made for Two #1533

ROXANN DELANEY

is the mother of four daughters. With the two oldest on their own, although a mere twenty yards away, life in her hometown in south-central Kansas is still far from dull. The 1999 Maggie Award winner enjoys keeping up with the former high school classmates she encounters and the tons of relatives, whose ancestors settled in the area over a century ago. A theater buff, she once helped establish a community theater and both acted and directed in the productions, as well as served on the board of directors. But writing is her first love, and she is thrilled to have followed the yellow brick road to the land of Silhouette Romance. She would love to hear from readers, who can write to her at P.O. Box 636, Clearwater, KS 67026.

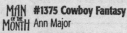

Chapter One

"Come on over here, sugar, and I'll show you what a real man can do."

Ignoring the remark coming from one of the drunken men near a row of stock trailers, Ellie Warren lifted her chin in an indignant gesture. She stomped past them, muttering to herself. "Stupid, brain-dead cowboy."

The smell of whisky, sweat and animals—some of them the two-legged variety—drenched the night air around the Cedar Rapids, Iowa, rodeo grounds. None of the aromas were new to Ellie. She'd spent the past twelve years, since she was fourteen, barrel racing and the last six of those traveling across the country. She had put up with all manner of rude and crude cowboys, and it hadn't taken her long to figure out the best way to deal with them. Ignore them.

Her muttering didn't cease as she wound her way through the contestant campgrounds behind the arena to her camper. "Oughta have their mouths filled with manure."

Exhaustion slowed her steps, and it took every ounce of energy she had to lift her dust-covered boot onto the metal platform at the back of her pickup camper. She needed a shower, but she'd rather wait until morning than go back through the huddle of men she'd skirted around in the darkness.

Sticking the key in the lock and turning the knob, she pulled open the door and stepped inside. She groped in the dark to switch on a light while she yanked her hat from her head. The hat fell to the countertop, and her gaze dropped to the floor.

Her blood-curdling scream, at the sight of the snake curled on the floor, bounced off the thin camper walls.

Thoughts skittered through her mind, but none made sense. Without taking her attention from the cold-blooded invader, Ellie acted on instinct and eased open the door of the small closet to her right. After carefully pulling out a newly purchased, flat-bottomed shovel, intended for her horse trailer, she jabbed the edge onto the snake as close to its head as possible. Praying the critter would stay put, she gripped the wooden handle with both hands and jumped atop the metal. The snake flipped and writhed beneath the blade, and Ellie realized what she'd just done. Frozen to the spot in shock and unable to move, except to brace herself with one hand against the cabinet for balance, a shudder shook her body.

Now what? she thought, when the snake slowed its wriggling. If she got off and it came after her, she'd die of fright. Mercy, she hated snakes! But staying propped on the shovel for eternity wasn't an option, either.

Her heart regained its beat, pounding ninety to nothing, and her breath came in quick, short bursts. Her knees were so weak and shaky she thought she'd fall off the only thing between her and her unwelcome guest. Taking a deep but unsteady breath, she tried to focus on her alternatives. There didn't seem to be any.

When the door banged open behind her, she let out another ear-splitting scream.

"What the hell's goin' on?" a deep baritone barked.

The shovel wobbled beneath her as she craned her neck to discover a pair of bright-blue eyes staring at her from beneath a black Stetson. She couldn't be certain if the cowboy's gaze was sliding over her or the shovel, but for the moment it didn't matter.

Swallowing the lump of fear lodged in her throat, she managed one word. "S-snake."

"Sure is," he said with a quirk of his lips. His gaze traveled back to hers. "You okay?"

Finding that her voice had deserted her, she nodded.

He stepped up into the camper and knelt down next to her. "Hang on."

Unable to watch, she squeezed her eyes shut. She could feel him grip the handle, then both she and the shovel tilted to the left and back again. He brushed against her leg, and another shudder shook her, this one warm instead of cold.

"It's just a bull snake, hon," he said, standing.

"Right. Just a snake." She gritted her teeth to keep them from chattering, but her terror eased when his soft chuckle swept through her like a hot, summer wind.

"You can get down, now."

Uncertain if it was completely safe to remove herself from the shovel, and afraid to look, she stayed put. "Are you sure? Is it...dead?"

"Naw. You aren't big enough to do that. You just kinda choked him up a little."

He stood so close to her his warm breath whispered across her temple. The shovel gained her nearly a foot in height, but when she opened her eyes, she still had to look up to see into his eyes.

She nearly fell off the shovel when she recognized her rescuer as Chace Brannigan, the nation's leading saddle bronc rider.

Sliding his arm around her waist, he held her steady. "One step at a time, hon."

She took another deep breath, forcing herself to ignore the way her heart skipped a beat, and eyed his other hand. The snake's body hung limp in his grip. "Get rid of that, will you?"

He glanced at the reptile before giving her a lopsided grin. "Soon as you get down from there."

The soft, rhythmic thumping of his heart against her shoulder sent her own heart pounding. His scent— fresh air and rugged country male—surrounded her, making her slightly dizzy. She knew she should be scrambling down, but she couldn't seem to set herself in motion. She'd encountered plenty of cowboys in her twenty-six years, but none had ever caused her heart to trip like a moonstruck adolescent's.

Determined to gain control of herself, Ellie stepped off the shovel. He didn't let go. The cramped interior of the camper was filled with the cowboy, making breathing difficult. Without room to take a step in any direction, she forced air into her lungs and out again until her head cleared.

"The snake?" she reminded him in a voice that didn't sound normal.

"Oh, yeah." He released her and took a step back to the door, tossing out the body, which had begun to move.

Shrinking away, she bit the inside of her cheek to keep from screaming again. While his attention was occupied, she pivoted around the shovel and put the implement between them, breathing only a little easier.

"Thanks," she said, when he'd pulled the door shut and faced her.

He shrugged, crossed his arms on his broad chest and leaned against the closet. "That's a dangerous weapon. You always keep a shovel handy?"

She kept her gaze averted from a pair of shoulders as wide as Texas, but she could feel him watching her. "It's safer in here."

"Couldn't be too safe, considering that snake."

She jerked her head up to stare at him. "What's that supposed to mean?"

"Snakes can crawl through some pretty small spaces," he said with a grin. "It coulda come up through a hole. Reckon you ought to double-check the place. Just in case." He shoved away from the closet, shrinking the space between them.

Nodding, she propped the shovel against the wall. Bone weary from the loss of adrenaline no longer pumping through her body, she took a step back on wobbly legs and sank onto the cushioned seat around the small table. "I'll do that."

"And you might want to keep your door locked. If I can come in, anybody can."

Ellie thought of the cowboy who had called out to her. "Dumb cowboys," she muttered.

"'Scuse me?"

Her cheeks burned when she realized what she'd said. The cowboy in front of her had saved her from what she considered a fate worse than death, and here she was insulting him and his kind.

"Sorry," she said, ducking her head. She managed to push herself to her feet. She didn't like being beholden to anyone, but she'd been raised with manners. Keeping her gaze on the pearl snaps of his colorful Western shirt, she stuck out her hand. "Thanks for...rescuing me. I guess I owe you."

One long stride brought him closer to her, and he took her hand, engulfing it in his. Being barely five feet tall had often put her at a disadvantage, but she'd dealt with it. Until now. He was one big cowboy. She reasoned that he wasn't any bigger than a dozen other cowboys she knew, but he sure seemed like it. Strength radiated from him, overpowering her senses and leaving her tongue-tied.

"My pleasure." His voice was a husky whisper.

When he didn't let go immediately, she slowly raised her gaze past the solid, muscled chest she'd leaned against, over a strong, chiseled chin and jaw. Lingering on lips set in a crooked smile, she looked up into twinkling eyes. That was enough to remind her of what was happening. What was she thinking?

She jerked her hand from his, leaving a tingling sensation in her fingers. She had more sense than to be mesmerized by a hunky cowboy with cool pools of blue for eyes. She'd had enough of cowboys and ranches to last her the rest of her life. And all of it learned at the price of her parents' lives. No, she was not looking for a cowboy. No way, no how.

"Well, thanks again," she said, hoping to get him out of the camper in a hurry.

He didn't budge. "You had a good ride tonight."

She shrugged, trying to relax in spite of the way he was looking at her. "Not bad."

"It was good enough to keep you ahead and win the first-place prize money. You're standing pretty high in the rankings."

Ellie nodded. A few more wins and she'd have a secure spot for the National Finals Rodeo in Las Vegas. Winning the Barrel Racing title wasn't important. She only wanted to compete. Once. And then she'd be done with it. Retired. She'd leave her gypsy life-style behind for an easy life in the city. Easier than going from rodeo to rodeo, at least. Much easier than living on the Oklahoma ranch her parents had left her and her brothers. A ranch she didn't want to return to. Ever.

"I'm really tired," she told the cowboy, when she realized he was still standing before her. "If you don't mind…"

"Oh. Yeah. Guess it is late." Hesitating, as if he'd just been shaken out of a deep sleep, he finally turned for the door, opened it and stepped down.

Ellie let out a sigh of relief, welcoming the breathing space his departure gave her. She was ready to collapse into bed—clothes, boots and all.

"Be sure and lock up," he reminded her, sticking his head back inside.

"I will." She waited for him to close the door, but he stood watching her. "As soon as you leave," she added as incentive.

"I'm Chace Brannigan."

"I know." Did he think she was deaf and blind?

Who didn't know Chace Brannigan? She'd heard of the three-time champion saddle-bronc rider and seen his pictures plastered in every rodeo magazine in the country, but their paths had never crossed. The roller-coaster ride her stomach was on made her wish they hadn't this time, either.

"Yeah, well, lock up," he said again.

With a sigh of exasperation, she glared at him. "I said I would."

"Now."

He disappeared, and the door swung shut with a thud. Ellie stared at it for a moment before forcing her feet to move. She always locked the door. Especially at night. She locked it to keep out cowboys like him.

"Lock the door," she mimicked under her breath. She could take care of herself and didn't need anyone telling her what to do. Peeling back the curtain at the window only enough to peek outside, she saw him standing on the ground less than a foot from her camper, watching the door.

"Just turn the little button," he prompted from the other side.

"I am!" She let the fabric slip from her fingers and, with an angry snap, turned the lock. "Satisfied?"

"Yep."

Even through the camper door she could hear his soft laughter, and the warmth of it spread through her. "Dumb cowboy," she whispered to ward it off.

Chace's shoulders shook with long-suppressed mirth as he made his way through the dimly lit camp-grounds. It felt good to laugh. Damn good. He couldn't remember the last time he'd found much of anything to more than chuckle over. But the sight of that little lady perched on that shovel, her eyes as big as silver dollars.... He laughed even louder. She'd reminded him of a stick of dynamite, ready to go off at any second.

The humor vanished, and a frown replaced his grin. How the hell had that snake gotten in her camper? It hadn't been poisonous, but it was no laughing matter. Most women were scared to death when they got within ten feet of a snake. And it was obvious that she traveled alone. Nobody to look out for her.

The thought brought him down faster than snow in an avalanche. If he had to, he'd make sure himself that her camper was secure. Besides varmints like that snake, some rodeoers were a shade on the rowdy side, especially as National Finals drew nearer. Lately he'd noticed some of them erring a little too far on the side of trouble. Another good reason to get out while he had a chance to finish on top.

And that list of reasons grew by the day. Dragging his aching body from bed each morning without someone's help was still possible, but it wasn't easy. He'd been kicked, stomped, thrown and just plain busted-up enough to make a decision. This was it, his last year—last chance—to have a double championship by winning the Saddle Bronc title and the All-Around Cowboy title with team roping. He'd been here before, a few years back, a little younger and a lot less hampered by injuries, but he'd missed winning both titles by a narrow margin. Being older and more experienced could give him a slight edge over the younger cowboys. But *slight* was stretching it. His riding and roping would have to be better than ever with no distractions.

He could do it, and then he'd head home to Texas

a big winner. He'd shirked his responsibilities to the family ranch long enough, and he was ready to fix that. Sending his winnings home wasn't enough anymore. His brother needed help with the place. Chace needed to be there. He wanted to be there.

As he neared his truck and horse trailer, the memory of the little bit of a woman came to mind again. Caramel-colored hair blended with chocolate-drop eyes to create a confection that tempted his sweet tooth. But damn, he was on a diet. No women until he had those gold buckles holding his belt together.

"Hey, Brannigan."

Squinting, Chace could see his traveling and team roping buddy leaning against the truck with one boot propped against the side of the door. "Ray."

"That last ride of yours was the best yet," his friend answered.

When he reached the truck, Chace pulled his bronc saddle out of the back. "Hope the next one's as good. Thanks for taking care of Redneck."

"No problem." Ray moved away from the door. "We gonna get a room, or what?"

Chace peered into the darkness in the direction of the camper he'd just left. "That little barrel racer, the one who beat out Cheryl. What's her name?"

Ray tipped his hat back. "Ellie Warren. She's one little bitty package."

"Good with the barrels, too," Chace agreed, thinking of her winning ride that night.

"Damn straight."

Chace didn't believe she was in any danger, but he did know she'd had a bad scare. It hadn't escaped him that the lock on her door was a sorry excuse for security. If one of the boys in the crowd near her truck

had been tipping the bottle a few too many times...
She might be dynamite, but she wasn't big enough to
handle a drunken cowboy.

"Think you can pull the truck into that spot over
there?" He pointed to a space barely able to accom-
modate his stretch-cab pickup.

Ray scratched at a day's growth of beard and shot
him a curious look. "Might be a problem with the
trailer."

"Unhook it. I've got to check on something. I'll
make sure the horses are settled when I'm done." He
opened the truck door, tossed in the saddle where it
would be safe from the elements and grabbed a piece
of baling wire from behind the seat.

"I'll throw the bedrolls in the back," Ray offered
as he opened the other door and slid behind the steering wheel.

"This won't take long."

Less than a minute later, Chace stood at Ellie's
camper door and rapped his knuckles hard on the alu-
minum. When he didn't get a response, he pounded
with his fist. From inside, he heard movement along
with muffled curses that would make any cowboy
proud.

"Who's there?"

"Chace Brannigan." The door flew open, forcing
him to jump back to keep from being smacked with
it.

Ellie stood in the opening with her fists planted on
her hips and a scowl on her face. "Now what?"

Her choice of sleeping attire caught him by surprise
and rendered him speechless. Boys' cotton pajamas
covered with brown bucking broncs on a tan background swallowed up her slight frame. The hem of the

arms covered her hands, and the legs pooled at her feet where bare toes peeked beneath the too-long cuffs.

Movement forced his attention up when she crossed her arms. The action revealed a fair amount of smooth, tanned cleavage where the front gaped open, and he couldn't stop looking.

"What's the matter? Haven't you ever seen a pair of pajamas?"

Chace swallowed.

"Well?"

"Not since I was eight years old. Not like...those." He forced a grin and hoped it didn't resemble a leer. Raising his gaze to lower the skyrocketing heat that threatened to cause him some embarrassment at any moment, he took in the angry line of compressed lips. Dark eyes flashed a warning, framed by unruly waves of silky hair from the braid she'd unleashed.

"What are you doing here, Brannigan?"

The ice in her voice brought him back to his senses. "The door."

Her foot tapped beneath the loose pajama fabric. "What about it?"

"Close it and lock it behind me."

"That's the most intelligent thing you've said." Her arms dropped to her sides, ending the display of sun-tanned flesh. Reaching out, she pulled the door shut, slamming it in his face.

He heard the snap of the lock and, "Good night, again, Mr. Brannigan."

Chuckling, he shook his head. He stuck the wire into the keyhole and wiggled it while he turned the handle.

"What in the name of heaven are you—" the door

pulled open to reveal her wide eyes and pale face
"—doing?"

"That lock might as well be a piece of tape." He
removed the wire and held it up to show her. "Baling
wire. Staple of any cowboy's life."

"I know that," she snapped.

"You're about as safe as—"

"I know that, too." Biting her lip, she sank back
against the counter and shook her head. Fear shimmered in her eyes. "Now what do I do?"

He stepped up and into the camper. "Long-term,
we put a sizable lock on that door."

"We?"

He shrugged. "Okay, *I'll* put a lock on it."

Her chin tilted up. "It's my camper. My home."

He considered her choice of words. "Maybe a home
security system—"

"Oh, for heaven's sake," she said in a huff, pushing
away from the counter. "I'll take care of it tomorrow."

The thought of someone so small sleeping un-
guarded made his head ache. "What about tonight?"

Her brows drew together in a thoughtful frown, and
one finger tapped her full lips.

"Hell's bells," he muttered at an imagined possession of those lips with his.

"Bells!" She spun around and bent over to dig
through a cabinet tucked at the base of the over-the-
cab sleeping area.

He bit back a groan and pried his gaze from the
view of horses galloping across her delectable behind.
He didn't look back again until he heard a loud, nerve-
rattling clang.

With a wide grin on her face, Ellie held up a large,

brass cowbell. She gave him a push toward the door. "I'll tie it on the doorknob. If anybody dares to touch that door during the night, I'll be up in a flash."

Considering how hard he'd had to knock, Chace doubted a shotgun blast would be enough to wake her, but he kept his opinion to himself. His truck was parked close enough that if the bell did ring, there'd be enough commotion to rouse him.

Her hand at his back, she gave him another shove. "Go on. Try it. But give me a second to get it tied on."

Clamping his mouth shut on the protest he knew she'd argue with, he stepped out into the quiet night and took a deep breath. Crisp air filled his lungs as he heard the far-from-melodic clunk of the bell hitting the door as it closed behind him.

"Okay, try it," she said from the other side.

He turned around and grabbed the knob, shaking it gently.

Clang. Clang.

The door opened a crack, and she peeked out at him, the bell jangling loud enough to wake the dead. "It works!" Her smile dimmed. "I guess I owe you…again."

"It was your idea," he reminded her.

She opened the door wider, her smile turning grateful. "Yeah, it was. But thanks for checking on the door. I wouldn't have known if you hadn't shown me."

He gazed at a figure that had to be a stretch to make five feet. His fingers itched to dip into the soft, buttery waves framing her face. Her features were as diminutive as the rest of her, except for the full, lush lips of her wide mouth and her enormous brown eyes. "My pleasure…again."

He made his way back to his truck, wondering how such a pint-size woman could cause the way-too-tight fit of his jeans. Hell, he was thirty-three years old. Old enough to be her… A dozen words crossed his mind— *brother, uncle, cousin*—but only one stuck. *Lover.*

"Forget it, Brannigan. She's a kid," he reminded himself while he checked his roping horse and Ray's. But his body told him she was a woman, in spite of her childlike size.

In the back of his pickup, he pulled his boots off and stretched out on the empty bedroll next to his buddy. Ignoring the snores, he folded his arms behind his head and studied the star-studded black sky. The night air held a definite chill he hoped would cool the flames licking at him. He needed to get his mind back on the business of rodeo. He'd never been responsible for anyone but himself. He'd be crazy to get involved with anything other than winning those buckles and saving his family's ranch, the Triple B—especially a woman.

Hell's bells, he thought with a sigh and a silent chuckle. What would the minibundle of trouble bring next?

The sound of pounding and a cowbell ringing jerked Ellie to a sitting position. With luck, she narrowly missed hitting her head on the low ceiling of the over-the-cab bed.

"What in tarnation is that awful racket?" joined the clanging of the bell.

A smile twisted Ellie's mouth at the sound of the

female voice announcing the identity of her visitor. "Hang on a sec, Reba."

The noise ceased as she scrambled from her loft. She reached the door and opened it to offer an apologetic smile. "Sorry about that."

A head of garish red hair preceded the plump, middle-aged woman into the camper. Her suspicious gaze landed on Ellie. "What's goin' on here?"

"It's a long story."

Shoving back the too-long sleeves of the pajamas she'd snitched from one of her brothers, Ellie tried to decide the best way to explain the bell without going into details. Until she could wake up completely and come to terms with what had happened last night and her ridiculous reaction to the cowboy, she didn't want to say too much.

Reba Tucker, kindhearted soul that she was, wouldn't take the news of the snake lightly. The woman had traveled the rodeo circuit with her steer-roper husband for too many years to let the incident slide by with nothing more than a comment or two. No, Reba would make a big fuss over it, and Ellie didn't want to deal with a hysterical mother hen.

And she didn't want to mention Chace Brannigan. That's all Reba would need to set her off on her favorite topic: Cowboys Make Great Husbands. Nate Tucker might be among the best of spouses, but Ellie didn't want a man who had Wrangler across his butt, or Justin's on his feet and a Stetson on his head. She didn't particularly want any man. She'd never needed one yet.

Dragging her fingers through her sleep-tangled hair, Ellie sighed. "I noticed the lock on my door isn't working right. Until I can have it checked out, the cowbell is a great alarm.''

Reba crossed her arms on her ample chest and leaned one hip against the counter. ''That's it? Dang, girl, all you had to do was say somethin' to Nate. He'd have skedaddled as fast as a rabbit with a hound dog on his tail to the nearest hardware store and had you snugged up like a baby in a blanket in no time.''

With a grateful smile, Ellie steered the conversation away from her jerry-rigged alarm system. ''Is Nate riding in Phoenix?''

Reba nodded. ''We're planning to stop at Laura's for a day to see my new grandbaby. You gonna compete after the cutoff date for Finals?''

''I may stop at the ranch. I can get some practice in there. And it may be the last time I get to see the place.''

Reba's mouth settled into a frown. ''It's your home, girl. Yours and your brothers. You aren't still plannin' to sell it, are you?''

But it hadn't been her home since she'd left it six years ago, when Matt turned eighteen, to travel the rodeo circuit. She had only returned when it was absolutely necessary, avoiding the memories she had trouble dealing with. She refused to let the ranch take her brothers' lives as it had their parents'. Once it was sold, maybe she could finally escape the past.

Gripping the edge of the counter with one hand, she gathered her determination. ''I'm selling. There won't be any more working themselves into an early grave.''

Reba placed her hand on Ellie's. ''That was a freak accident that took your folks. That sorta thing don't happen—''

''Ranching is a back-breaking, money-sucking way

of life." Ellie pulled away as gently as possible and shoved aside the painful memory of her parents. She couldn't bear to think about the accident except to remind her that she had to make sure nothing like it would ever happen to the boys.

"They're adults, Ellie. Let them make their own decisions."

"I know that. I finished raising them after the folks—" Ellie stopped and took a deep breath. "I know the dangers of ranching. I can't let anything happen to them. Especially after Matt broke his collarbone last year. It could've been worse. Much worse."

"You weren't even lookin' to sell the place," Reba pointed out as she'd done several times.

Ellie sighed and looked away. It was turning into the same old tiresome argument. Reba couldn't see the dangers she did. There were too many things that could happen to her brothers on the ranch. And too many memories for her. Next, Reba would ask what she planned to do. Other than move to the city, she didn't have an answer. Getting the boys off the ranch came first. After that, she'd worry about how to support herself. If she could qualify for National Finals, she might make enough money to see her way clear. For a while.

"I guess I'd better get the trailer hooked up," she said without looking at her friend. "It's past time to get on the road."

"Nate's probably wonderin' where I've got off to," Reba said, letting the subject drop, and turned for the door. "You take care until Phoenix. We'll see you there."

"You bet."

When Reba had gone, Ellie opened the closet door

to reach for a towel. Catching her reflection in the full-length mirror on the inside of the door, she stared at the image looking back at her and grimaced.

"No wonder Chace Brannigan was gawking at you last night," she announced to the rumpled figure before her. Turning sideways, she grabbed at the back of the excess pajama fabric to pull it tight across her body and scrutinized the effect.

With a disgusted grunt, she released the material. What did she care if she didn't have the kind of curves men panted over?

She quickly changed into her clothes from the night before and grabbed a clean set, ready to hit the showers and eager to get on the road. But when she pushed open the camper door, the first thing she saw was the cowboy who'd rescued her the night before. He was obviously headed for the showers, a towel draped around his neck.

When he didn't look her way, she breathed a sigh of relief and ducked into the camper. Ignoring the clippity-clop of her heart, she waited until she felt safe to leave.

She wasn't interested in a cowboy, couldn't be, even if he was the current leading saddle bronc rider in the country and sexy as sin, to boot. She knew all about his kind. She'd met too many "my way or no way" cowboys. Hadn't she proven she could do it alone? Besides, rodeoers ended up on ranches. She wanted desperately to leave the past and that kind of life behind. Nothing would stop her. And she didn't need anyone's help. The sooner she got on the road, the sooner she could put some distance between herself and one particular, bossy cowboy.

Chapter Two

Bleary-eyed from too little sleep, Chace let the sting-ing spray of the primitive shower near the arena clear the fog from his brain. To his disgust, his sharper mind left him with vivid memories of the night before.

"Hell," he muttered when his body began to spring to life. He'd spent half the night listening for the clang of a bell and the other half considering a cold shower. There were other remedies for his problem. One idea, which included hauling a particular petite package into his arms, he promptly discarded. Reviewing every millisecond of his latest ride in his mind would be safer. And damn sure more productive.

Dressed again and whistling an off-key tune, he started for his truck. As soon as Ray returned with a thermos of coffee, they'd be on the road. With barely a month to go until the official end of the season, Chace was eager to get to Phoenix. After that, only a few more rodeos until National Finals. Then, if every-thing went well, he could retire. The money he hoped to win would keep the Triple B Ranch in the black and put an end to worrying about losing it. That, and stop his youngest brother's plans to turn the family spread into a dude ranch. Hell, he didn't want strangers traipsing all over the place.

Once back home again, he could begin to make up for leaving Trey to deal with the ranch on his own. Maybe they'd even get lucky enough to entice their brother, Dev, to come home. Working together, they could keep it out of the wrong hands and make the place the successful ranch it had once been. Four generations of Brannigans had owned and worked the Triple B, and he and his brothers had fought to keep it after their father's death. He knew he belonged there. He'd ducked his responsibilities for too long.

Wide awake, and with his hormones under control and well leashed, Chace didn't bother to steer clear of Ellie's camper. But he didn't expect to find temptation in a tank top as she leaned over to hook her horse trailer to her pickup, offering him a much better glimpse than the pajama top had the previous night.

"Hell and damnation," he grumbled, knowing that's exactly what he was in for if she didn't straighten up and change the view.

To his relief, she moved, but only to the opposite side of the trailer hitch, giving him an eyeful of worn denim stretched tight across the best-looking little backside he'd seen in a long time. It was even better without the pajama horses galloping across it. The sight pulled a tortured groan from him. If he had any sense, he'd turn around and walk back to his truck and forget all about it. But his feet wouldn't move away any faster than his eyes.

As he watched her wrestle with the coupling, he

clenched his hands into fists. He had to do something besides stand there with his tongue hanging out like a panting dog. When she gave the bumper an angry kick, he moved into action.

"I'll get it," he growled.

Her head jerked up, her eyes wide but narrowing as he closed the gap between them. "I can do it," she announced, giving him her back and bending over again.

Beads of sweat popped out on his forehead when he stopped behind her. All he had to do was take hold of those mind-blowing curves and pull her up against him. He placed his hands on her hips, but forced himself to scoot her aside. "Let me do it."

"It's my rig," she said in a tight voice from behind him while he gave the hitch a nudge.

"And it'll be your smashed fingers," he replied, snapping the ball cover in place. He turned to find her slipping into a faded chambray shirt and noticed her hands tremble as she fought the buttons.

Anger? He hoped not. He wanted to have the same effect on her that she had on him. It would serve her right.

With her head down and her face hidden from view, her fingers fumbled with the last button. "I've been managing my own truck and trailer for almost ten years, since I was old enough to drive. I've hooked them up thousands of times."

He detected a tremor in her voice, but when her head came up and she looked at him, he saw the flash of defiance in her eyes. Damn, she was one stubborn woman.

"Look, Brannigan, I appreciate what you did for me last night, but I don't need your help. I can take care of myself. Just let me get loaded and on the road.'' She did a quick pivot and marched to untie her horse from the back of a nearby truck.

He moved out of her way and leaned back against the side of the trailer, watching in silence as she loaded her horse into her trailer with the skill of a seasoned professional. Maybe she didn't need his help now, but without it the night before, no telling what she would have done. Her gentle handling of her horse proved she wasn't as tough as she might want him to believe. And the stubborn tilt of her chin as she stomped past him to the cab of her truck didn't erase the memory of the terror he'd seen in her eyes the previous night. It only aggravated him.

He stalked to the truck's door, reaching it as she slammed it shut with such force it could have registered on the Richter Scale. Planting his hands on the edge where the window was rolled down, he leaned in, his face inches from hers. ''You may not want my help, but you sure as hell need it.''

A red flush flooded her cheeks, and her chin went up another notch. ''Get your face out of my truck,'' she said in a haughty tone.

''Now look here, little bit, I got rid—''

''Don't!'' The crimson shade of her face went deathly pale. Tears glistened in her dark eyes, and she squeezed them shut. ''Don't ever call me that.''

Reaching in, he cradled her cheek in his hand. ''Aw, hon, I didn't mean to—''

''Leave me alone,'' she whispered. ''Please.'' When her lids fluttered open, she turned her head, slipping away from him, and she reached for the ignition. Gunning the motor, she slammed the truck into gear, spewing dirt behind her tires and nearly taking his head and hand with her.

Chace stood staring after her. What the hell had he done? Was his touch so repulsive to her? No, it hadn't been that. He'd felt her lean into his palm, felt her tremble in his hand. Then dammit, why would she shake him off like water on a wet dog?

He made his way to his own truck and trailer, cursing himself for caring when she obviously wasn't interested. He'd forget about her by the time he got to Phoenix.

But once on the road, he found it harder than he'd thought to rid himself of her reaction to his touch and his body's response. Five hundred miles later, with Ray jabbering away the entire trip, Chace wished he'd asked her where she'd be riding next. He had a few questions, when and if he caught up with her. And he'd damn well get some answers.

Ellie pulled her rig in behind the arena near Phoenix just after noon on Friday. She'd made good time, but a week on the road, even though she hadn't rushed, left her exhausted. Sometimes it was more tiring than the competing.

Each weekend she competed somewhere, earning or not earning enough to place among the top fifteen money winners by the end of the season. Only those placing qualified for the National Finals Rodeo in Las Vegas, held the first week of each December. As soon as she finished in Phoenix, she'd head for Austin to do the same thing again. And again, until she hopefully made it to Finals. There would be a month break before that first week in December, but she wasn't looking forward to it. This time she couldn't avoid going home.

Home. Ellie sighed and climbed out of her pickup to check on Sky Dancer, thinking of that long month in Oklahoma looming ahead. The thought brought back the old panic and guilt. But she didn't have a choice. She loved her two brothers and wanted to see them both happy. And safe. Alive and not old before their time. It would take getting them off the ranch to do that. And that meant selling the place, no matter what they thought they wanted. She knew best. Now that she had a prospective buyer, she only had to convince Matt and Brett to sign the papers.

After securing her camper with the new lock she'd had installed, she took Sky Dancer out of the trailer. Her boots kicked up dust in the dry grass as she worked. Rain had been scarce in the area, but from previous experience she knew the arena was well tended. She could concentrate on her riding.

She saddled and bridled Sky Dancer to give him some exercise and herself a welcome break from being behind the wheel. Seeing Reba and Nate's truck and trailer pull into the lot, she reminded herself to stop on the way back to say howdy. Rodeoers were like a close-knit family. But after spending over half her life competing, she wanted a change—new faces, new experiences. That was for the future. All she wanted for the moment was to relax and ease the knots from her shoulders. Her ride tonight wouldn't be worth spit if she couldn't loosen up.

When she'd put enough distance between herself and the parking area, she urged Sky Dancer into a gallop. It should have done the trick, but she couldn't get a particular cowboy out of her mind. The touch of his hand on her cheek had brought a comfort she'd almost forgotten existed, until she'd realized how weak and vulnerable it made her. She couldn't allow it. She'd been on her own since raising her brothers— a job she'd finished without help from anyone. She couldn't start needing someone now, not when she was so close.

By the time she returned to the campgrounds, it was well past two. Hoping to catch Reba, she guided Sky Dancer to the Tuckers' trailer.

Before she could dismount, Reba appeared in the doorway. "You made good time."

"How was Laura?"

"Busy." Reba wiped her hands on her jeans and frowned. "Timmy and little Sally were stayin' with friends, and the new baby was colicky. Wouldn't even let me hold him."

Ellie felt her friend's disappointment. "Next time he'll be better."

With a hopeful smile Reba dug into her pockets and sighed when her hands came up empty. "I'm out of ice, and I always have a glass of cold tea ready for Nate 'fore he heads out for the evenin'. Would you mind gettin' me a bag at the concession stand?"

"Not at all," Ellie replied.

"Let me fetch some money." Reba ducked back inside.

While Ellie waited, the area filled with a variety of vehicles, and she waved to the people she recognized. When a hand rested on her thigh, she nearly bolted from her saddle, spooking Sky Dancer and forcing her to concentrate on calming him.

"Get the door fixed?" a deep, familiar voice asked.

Her heartbeat accelerated as she turned to look down at Chace Branningan. "Are you following me?"

His grin was enough to melt the polar ice cap. "Nope. Didn't know we were destined to run into each other so soon."

"Disappointed?" she asked, and watched an assortment of emotions cross his face.

Pure devilment won out to dance in his eyes. "Miss me?"

Ellie wasn't about to admit she'd thought of little else other than him and the sale of the ranch over the six days she'd spent on the road. "I completely forgot we met."

The light in his eyes flashed, and he shot her a devilish grin. "Yeah. I know the feeling."

"A ten-pound bag shouldn't be more than—" Reba's voice halted, and Ellie turned in the saddle to look at her. Her gray-eyed gaze drifted to Chace and back again to Ellie, and her mouth turned up in a Cheshire Cat smile. "I'll get the ice."

"No," Ellie said in a rush and turned to scowl at Chace. "Mr. Brannigan was just leaving." Having Reba see them together, no matter how innocent, was a bad idea. No telling what the woman might get in her head.

"Haven't seen you for a while, Chace," Reba said, her grin widening. "I didn't know you two knew each other.

He looked at Ellie and offered another knee-weakening grin before turning back to Reba. "I had the pleasure of meeting her last week in Cedar Rapids."

"Really? In that case, why don't I fix us all lunch

tomorrow and you can get better acquainted. Say at noon?''

With a grin, he touched the brim of his hat. ''That sounds mighty fine.''

Ellie shot her friend a murderous look. He was the last person she wanted to spend time with. ''I'll be there if I can make it,'' she hedged. ''Keep your money, Reba. I'll get the ice.''

Without a glance at Chace, she nudged her horse toward the concession stand. Behind her, she could hear his soft chuckle, and she tightened her grip on the reins. Her day had taken a turn for the worst when he'd shown up. She hadn't expected to see him again, and with the season nearly over, the thought had both cheered and disappointed her. That alone was enough to worry her.

Her wait in line at the concession stand was blessedly short, and she added two candy bars, knowing Reba's penchant for chocolate.

Balancing the bag of ice on the saddle horn in front of her with one hand and holding the reins in the other, she wove her way through the gathering groups toward the Tuckers' trailer. She called a greeting over her shoulder to one of the other barrel racers, wishing her luck, and turned back when Sky Dancer came to a sudden halt.

Chace stood at the horse's head, holding the bridle and murmuring to the animal. Ellie opened her mouth to tell him to get lost, but when he looked at her, the words escaped her.

''Trying to avoid me?''

She knew she lacked the subtlety of most women, and his question brought the heat of embarrassment to her cheeks. ''N-no, of course not.''

Smoothing his hand along the horse's neck, Chace moved closer, never taking his eyes from hers. "What did I do to scare you off?"

Lifting her chin, she gripped the saddle horn and squeezed the ice, barely noticing the chill. It wasn't him that scared her, but what he did to her. She'd never met a man who could scramble her senses with a simple smile. And she'd met plenty of men, rodeo being a predominantly male sport. But no matter how much Chace made her nerves tingle and her mind go blank with just a look, he wasn't the man for her. She'd sworn off cowboys long ago. If she ever settled down, it wouldn't be with a vagabond rodeoer.

"I'm not afraid of you."

"But you don't like me much." His frown was formidable but didn't mask his puzzlement.

The confusion in his eyes tugged at her heart. "I really don't know you, so how can I tell?"

"We can fix that."

The air around her thickened, and her heart pounded. He hadn't moved, but somehow he seemed closer. There was nothing worse than a cowboy who couldn't take a hint, she reminded herself. And she'd done more than hint at him. She hated being rude, but he brought out the worst in her, stirring her up and leaving her with no choice.

Her hands shaking, she gathered the reins to leave, and the ice started to topple. Before she could react, Chace made a grab for it and settled it in the crook of his arm.

When she reached down to snatch it away, he took her hand and placed it on the horn, covering it with his. "If you weren't in such an all-fired hurry to get away from me..."

Ellie held her breath, ready to deny she wanted to avoid him, but with his hand on hers she couldn't find the words.

Letting go, he drew back and smiled, but it didn't reach his eyes. "I don't know what it is, little bit, but I intend to find out."

Opening her mouth to ask him what he meant, she froze at the sound of the nickname he'd called her again and squeezed her eyes shut. A vision of her dad lifting her onto a pony flashed through her mind. She swallowed, forcing back the memory that still caused a deep pain. It would only lead to more memories she couldn't deal with. "I told you not to call me that."

His hand returned to hers. "It slipped out. But you are—"

"Don't." She opened her eyes to see him studying her.

"You don't like anybody pointing out that you're on the small side?"

She shook her head. "It's not that. Call me shrimp, call me shorty, call me *tiny*. Just don't call me... *that*."

Chace tipped his head to one side before removing his hand. "Okay. If you promise to be there tomorrow for lunch at Reba's."

She bit back a scathing retort at his persistence. "You don't give up, do you?"

He shrugged and looked off in the distance. "You were the one who said you didn't know me well enough to know if you liked me. I don't see any reason why we can't be friends."

Ellie knew of plenty. One in particular. A big one. But she couldn't tell him that it was because of the heat he caused to pool in the area of her body closest to the saddle horn. "I guess there isn't," she fibbed.

"Good. Give it your best tonight." He handed her the ice and touched Sky Dancer on his rump, sending them on their way.

Sky Dancer shied as they circled the back of Reba's trailer. Ellie quickly regained control, but wondered if he'd needed a longer run.

"I was beginning to worry."

J. R. Staton was walking toward her, and she breathed a sigh of relief at the sight of her real estate agent. Handing him the ice, she offered a smile. "Give this to Reba while I tie up, would you?"

"I've had a new offer for the ranch," he said before turning to walk around the corner of the trailer, out of sight.

Ellie made quick work of sliding off her horse and making sure he was tethered, then she looked around to make sure Chace wasn't anywhere in sight. She didn't want to have to deal with him right now. This was far more important.

Talking about the sale, especially if it involved more money for her brothers, was much better than thinking about a wandering cowboy who turned her insides into a blazing bonfire.

The look on Reba's face when Ellie approached with J.R. was enough to ice down any flames she'd been feeling. Reba didn't like J.R. and took every opportunity to tell her so. J.R. wasn't a cowboy—the one thing that raised him in Ellie's estimation. She hadn't expected to hear from him, much less see him, until the break before Finals. But now that he was here, she was eager to get the latest news.

"Thanks for gettin' the ice," Reba said, taking the bag and planting herself in the doorway.

"It's nice to see you, Mrs. Tucker," J.R. said with a pained smiled.

Reba sniffed as she settled more firmly against the doorjamb. "You're a long way from home."

Ellie bit back a groan. She could have saved them the awkwardness if she'd known J.R. planned to be in the area.

He met Ellie's gaze and held it. "I have business in Phoenix, but I wanted to see Ellie first." He glanced at Reba who stood frowning at him. "To discuss the sale of the ranch, of course."

When Reba started to reply, Ellie rushed to trample anything she might say. "You said you had a new offer, J.R.?"

He nodded and focused his attention on her. "The buyer has decided the property may be worth more than first assumed. It's a good offer. I encourage you to accept it."

When he flashed her a smile, Ellie waited for the same sensations to overtake her that she felt when Chace Brannigan grinned at her. There wasn't even a twinge. Uneasy with the revelation, she shoved it aside. "All I'm asking is a fair price."

"We can discuss it further, on the way to your camper."

Reba looked heavenward and shook her head, giving Ellie the opportunity to escape. "I'll see you tomorrow, Reba."

"Noon, for lunch," her friend called after her, making it sound more like a command than a reminder.

"About the new offer," Ellie said, as she and J.R. walked to her camper.

He named a figure. She didn't know what to do. The amount he tossed out so cavalierly was still short of what she hoped to get. If there was the slightest chance that whoever wanted the ranch might go higher, she had to wait. The buyer had given two offers. Wasn't the third time charmed?

"Maybe the buyer will raise the offer," she suggested.

He pressed his lips together, and drew his brows down in a concerned frown. "I must caution you not to wait too long. This buyer is interested now. If you don't make a decision soon…"

"I want to speak with my brothers in person, at the ranch. I'll know more then."

His eyebrows arched and he opened his mouth to speak. Instead of saying anything, he closed it and nodded. "I have something for you in my car. I'll be right back."

Ellie smiled to herself as she watched him walk away. If she could put him off long enough, she'd have time at the ranch to persuade her brothers to see things her way. In the meantime maybe the buyer would up the price.

She wanted to retire after Finals. Even if she made enough to qualify, it wouldn't be enough to entice her brothers off the ranch. She had to sell it. But her brothers had to agree to the sale. And she didn't look forward to telling them about it.

After checking on the horses and making sure his gear would be ready and waiting before his first ride, Chace started out for the stock pens to look over the bronc he'd drawn. A good ride would keep him in the lead. A great one could give him an edge.

His path took him through the thickest of the parking area, and his thoughts, once again, turned to Ellie. He'd hoped she'd be here in Phoenix, but he hadn't counted on it. There were too many other places to compete. He'd spent most of the day wondering why he wanted to see her again, finally deciding that it was her downright stubbornness to fall for his charm that he found so attractive. What man could walk away from a challenge like that?

He smiled when he thought of the lucky break. But realizing how much it pleased him, he brought himself up short.

Had he gone loco? With four rodeos to go before the end of the season, he didn't need to form any kind of attachment to a woman. This late in the game, a female was a distraction he couldn't afford. He'd learned that the hard way, early on in his career, and knew better than to let it happen. He and the other three leaders were so close he couldn't let up much until after the final ride of the season. Concentration was the key. One slip up, one bad fall because his mind wasn't fully on his ride, and he might as well kiss his chance at any title goodbye. That wouldn't help the Triple B. As the oldest, it was his responsibility to see that the ranch prospered. They couldn't lose it the way they nearly had once. Mistakes and distractions were out of the question.

When he spied Ellie's pickup and camper to his left, he made a decision. He might be attracted to the miniature ball of fire, but he hadn't lost his mind. She'd told him flat-out that she didn't want him around. He'd been fool enough to let his body rule his brains. And he was getting too old to do that. No more. He'd steer clear of her from here on out.

Before he had a chance to backtrack and change his route, he saw Ellie approaching her camper. He stopped in midstride. She wasn't alone. He had a brief glimpse of a man with her, wearing a white shirt and tie, and carrying a suit coat slung over his shoulder. A cold hard ball of busted pride lodged in Chace's gut when he saw the bouquet of flowers in her hand. He'd been a bigger fool than he'd thought. She already had a man, and by the look of him, a simple rodeo cowboy would fail to measure up. Even if the cowboy won a dozen National Championships.

Disgusted with himself, Chace dared a last glance at the couple before he moved on to the stock pens. What he saw made his blood run cold, then hot. "Son of a—"

Ellie stood propped against the side of her camper gazing up at the last man he'd expect to see at a rodeo.

"Maybe a little competition from the right man would improve her eyesight."

Chace spun around to see Reba approaching. He would gladly give James Robert Staton a lot of things, including a shiner he owed him, but he remembered his decision to stay away from Ellie Warren. "Find another man, Reba. I've got a double championship to take care of, not a pint-size bundle of fireworks—who doesn't like me—to tangle with."

A glance at her told him she would hang on to this crazy idea she had like a dog with an old bone if he didn't set her straight. Sighing, he shook his head. "Not this time, Reba. You keep this to yourself, but this is my last year. I go out in a blaze of glory or I go out a loser."

Reba patted his arm with one plump hand. "You'll

never be a loser, Chace Brannigan. It's not in you. But that man is nothin' but trouble.''

Chace almost choked on his reply when he saw the object of their conversation reach out to push back a stray strand of Ellie's hair that had escaped her braid. "What do you mean?"

Reba's eyes flashed with impatience. "You're a man. Figure it out."

Chace didn't want to consider the implication of her words. Just watching Ellie conjured up an image of rumpled sheets and passion-drenched nights. Everybody else might see her as Ellie, a diminutive tomboy on a horse, taking barrels like the champ she would someday be. But Chace's eyes and body told him her dynamite temper and obstinate attitude hid something deeper. A passion he hoped to unleash and, at the same time, prayed he wouldn't.

When he turned around, Reba was gone. He had to make a decision. In spite of his earlier vow to stay away from the little spitfire, he wasn't about to let the man he'd known as Jimmy Bob since they were kids pull any of his con man tricks on her. Ellie needed protecting. And Chace was the man to do it.

Chapter Three

"What's wrong?" Ellie asked, when J.R. started to walk away in the middle of their conversation.

He turned back to her with a smile. "I thought I saw someone I know."

She tucked a strand of hair behind her ear and studied him. "Do you know many rodeo people?"

"One or two. Through business."

A small shiver of excitement rippled through her. Spending all of her life on the ranch, and then on the circuit, had isolated her from the rest of the world. No matter what she decided to do with herself after she retired, she wanted to see how nonrodeo people lived. And live it herself.

He touched her hand. "I'll be back to watch you ride. And tomorrow night when you're finished, we'll have dinner. But right now I need to get back to business."

Ellie ignored the fact that her heart didn't flutter at the physical contact. He had the oddest eyes. Brown, like hers, and almost impossible to read. With most people she knew what they were feeling by looking into their eyes, but his seldom showed emotion. Was he coming on to her?

"I'll see you tonight. I'll be cheering you on," he said, giving her hand a squeeze.

She thanked him and watched him walk away, unsure of what had transpired. But she didn't have time to dwell on it. If she didn't hurry, she'd be late. The sun had begun its descent on the horizon, and she needed to change before the opening ceremony. She'd never been much for the fancy outfits some of the others wore, but she made concessions, knowing the crowd liked to see the competitors in bright colors. The flashier, the better.

In her camper she stripped off her boots, jeans and shirt and opened the door to her closet. Reaching for her favorite deep-red, fringed shirt, she glanced in the mirror.

She'd never paid much attention to her body and couldn't remember the last time she'd taken a long look at herself. Being smaller than most women, she'd assumed she was still built like a young girl. The image of the woman in front of her gave her a completely different view. To her surprise she had hips, though nothing to brag about. Her larger-than-she'd-thought bust was nothing to write home about, either, but at least she had one. She straightened her shoulders and sucked in a breath. Not bad, she thought. But why hadn't she ever noticed?

"Because you never had a reason to care, you fool," she reminded her reflection. She took a step back for a better look. "Would men like this?" She'd had her share of wolf whistles from leering cowboys, but she'd brushed them off as matter-of-fact. That's the way cowboys were. When they got to know her, most of them treated her the same way her brothers did. None of them had ever had that spark of fire in their eyes that she'd seen in—

She shook her head. "Uh-uh, no way, girl. Don't even go there." Thinking of that particular cowboy was dead wrong. Pushy, arrogant and nothing but a rodeoer who'd wander for the rest of his life, Chace was a danger she couldn't let herself consider.

But why was it him who sent rivulets of heat through her whenever he looked at her? She might not know much about men, and she might not have paid much attention to her blossoming body, but she knew enough about both to know that he was the one who stoked a fire in her. She'd heard of chemistry, of how a woman's body reacted to some men. But chemistry wouldn't get her a home in the city and the kind of life she wanted. Chemistry would get her trouble.

Her pristine white bra and panties drew her attention. She remembered seeing fellow barrel racer, Dawn Dawson, in the showers in Memphis. The two of them were the same age, but Dawn had the body of Venus de Milo, and men always followed her around. The woman had peeled off her clothes right in front of Ellie, who had more modesty than she knew what to do with, to reveal jade-green bikini underwear and a matching bra that left little to the imagination.

Is that what makes Dawn's hips sway from side to side? What gives her such confidence?

Ellie took a step back and studied her reflection. Would fancy underthings help? Not that anyone would see them, of course. But only to know that a secret lay hidden beneath her jeans and shirts...?

It was a thought she pondered for some time.

Chace waited until J.R. had driven away before making his first move. If the weasel was on the scent of something that would gain him more than a few bucks, he wouldn't waste time. Chace needed to talk to Ellie and find out what she had that Jimmy Bob wanted. Things would only get worse if he put it off.

When the doorknob to her camper turned with ease, he swore under his breath, prepared to give her the blistering lecture she deserved. Hell, she'd already found one snake in there. Did she want to find another, this time with legs?

He wrenched open the door and leaped up the step. "When the hell are you going to—"

Freezing on the spot, his tirade stuck in his throat. Ellie stood less than five feet in front of him dressed in nothing but her unmentionables and looking at him with horror-filled eyes. He couldn't have stopped his body's reaction at the sight of her if someone had tossed a bucket of ice water on him. He'd seen women in less, but something about the maidenish look of Ellie did things to him he wouldn't have imagined.

Her mouth worked, but nothing came out, then she ducked behind an open door. "What the h-heck do you think you're doing, barging in here?"

He couldn't form the words to explain. He couldn't look away, either.

She peeked out from around the edge of the door and shot him a glare that should have done what ice water wouldn't have.

The fury on her face reminded him of his unfinished warning. "Don't you have enough sense to lock that door? Or didn't you get it fixed?"

"I got it fixed. I just don't think I need to lock it all the time," she stormed back. "Only *you* would have the nerve to come charging in here without knocking."

He ignored her comment on his manners, too angry with her for not locking up and worried that something could have happened to her. "Think again, Ellie. You travel alone. Anybody who wanted to could walk in at any time."

When her face lost all color, he felt like a heel. She disappeared from view, and he could hear her banging around in what he assumed was a closet. When she reappeared in a man's bathrobe that was a good five sizes too big for her, he had to clamp his teeth together to keep from bursting out laughing. She looked like a little girl playing dress-up in her daddy's clothes. But the little-girl image in his mind vanished when she turned to close the door, giving him a glimpse of one shapely bare leg. His breath caught, and the camper felt several square feet smaller.

"I suppose you're right," she admitted with a reluctant sigh. "But I doubt someone would bother in broad daylight."

"Don't underestimate a slightly deranged cowboy. Some of those boys start drinking long before the sun goes down." He didn't add that he was having trouble trusting himself and, as far as he knew, he wasn't deranged yet.

He wished he had his own strong drink when Ellie sat at the table. He stared, dry-mouthed and dumbstruck, as she pulled the edges of the robe to cover her crossed legs and smoothed a trembling hand over the fabric. The need to feel her caressing him the same way tightened his chest so badly he could barely breathe. He wanted to make her body tremble the way her hand did, to have her silky legs wrapped around him until—

He jerked his gaze up to hers when the sound of her voice broke through his fantasy. "What?"

"I asked you what you're doing here."

He moved his head from side to side, his gaze dropping to her lips. Lush, perfect lips, begging for his. For once, they weren't drawn in an angry frown. He had to get some control before he lost his mind and forgot what he'd come to say to her. He was here to protect her from an animal, but he was acting like one himself.

But the reminder didn't do the trick. Unable to keep his hands off her any longer, he caught her shoulders and pulled her to her feet. "Ellie—"

"Am I pretty, Chace?"

The sound of his name from her lips sent a shiver of heat straight through him to pool low. Pretty? Didn't she know? From the wide, questioning innocence in her dark eyes, he knew she didn't. It was long past time somebody told her.

"You're beautiful," he whispered, lowering his head for the kiss he needed more than air. But before he could touch his lips to hers, she pulled away, turning her back to him.

"That's a pretty far stretch, Brannigan," she said with a shaky laugh. "I bet you tell all the barrel racers the same thing."

He'd never said anything like that to any woman. He wasn't a man who whispered pretty words. But he doubted Ellie would believe him if he denied it, so he kept quiet.

She faced him, her smile forced and doubt in her

eyes. "And speaking of barrel racing, I was getting dressed when you bulldozed your way in here."

The mood was broken. He'd nearly blown it and had forgotten about his reason for wanting to talk to her. "Is your city slicker friend going to be watching you ride?"

Her smile disappeared. "You saw him?"

"On my way to check out my draw," he said with a casualness he didn't feel. Not when it came to Jimmy Bob Staton.

"Oh." She moved to the other side of the table and shrugged. "He's a business acquaintance."

"You've known him long?"

She shook her head. "A few months."

"Not long enough to trust him."

Her sharp intake of air should have warned him he'd missed another beat in this little two-step they were doing.

"Longer than I've known you. Look, Brannigan," she said, planting her hands on her hips, "I appreciate the help you've given me, but I don't need it. If I ever should, I'll let you know. But don't count on it."

If the decidedly feminine gesture hadn't reminded him that she was all woman, the acres of creamy skin it revealed would have. He had to get his mind back on the reason he was here. He needed to warn her about Jimmy Bob. But if he pushed it now, she'd have him out the door and on his butt in a flash, despite her size. Whether she wanted his help or not, she needed him. Not the same way he needed her to quench the fire she'd built in him since Iowa, but maybe even more.

He didn't dare look at her any longer. Keeping his

eyes on the toes of his boots, he moved to the door. "Guess I'll go saddle up."

"As long as it's your horse and not mine."

He swung around, hoping to see a smile on her face to tell him she was joking. Her scowl squashed that idea.

He touched the brim of his hat, not wanting to argue. It wouldn't do any good. "See you later."

"Don't count on it," she replied as he reached for the door handle. "I have a—plans."

When he looked over his shoulder at her, he couldn't miss seeing the flowers she'd stuck in a glass and left on the table. "With that guy in the suit, I suppose."

Her eyes blazed with anger. "Mind your own business, Brannigan, and let me take care of mine."

He didn't want to get involved, but he didn't have a choice. She was headed for disaster, and he had to stop her. *Now,* he urged himself. *Now, before it's too late.* "I know—"

"You know nothing," she cut him off.

"Then tell me—"

"I may be small, but I can take care of myself. And if I don't, I have two brothers who will. Contrary to what you might think, I know what I'm doing."

"Now, Ellie—"

"Out." She raised her arm and pointed to the door. The sleeves of her robe slid down her hand, over her fingers, diminishing the effect.

He came close to taking the few short steps it would take to reach her. She might have a streak of wildcat running through her, but a kiss would have her tamed in no time. If not, he could turn her over his knee and give her something to think about. But he did neither.

With a last look he hoped would stick in her mind, he left the camper.

She had him over a barrel. He'd planned to make a play for her. Distract her. And, if he were honest with himself, not just because of Jimmy Bob. He needed to find out what the attraction was, why Jimmy Bob was after her.

The Staton-Brannigan feud had gone on for four generations, and Jimmy Bob had lost. He hadn't taken it with much grace, either. But it hadn't stopped him. He still hadn't backed down. He was just waiting for the chance to grab the Triple B. All of it, not just what had once been Staton land.

Until then, Jimmy Bob had gone on to other pickings. There'd been stories of how he'd conned people, but never proof. Chace was waiting to get something rock solid on him. Once he had it, justice would be swift. He owed his family that much.

But when it came to Ellie, he couldn't stand by and do nothing, even if that's what she wanted. He needed to find a way to head off the disaster. If she was meeting Jimmy Bob after the rodeo, he had to do something, before things took a turn for the worse.

Ellie didn't notice the rider draw alongside her in the opening ceremony. Her mind was on her earlier encounter with Chace. It should have been on her upcoming race, but though she tried to steer her thoughts in that direction, she couldn't. And it wasn't making her happy.

"Evenin', Ellie."

The velvety baritone slid into her and joined her blood to flow through her veins. She didn't need to turn her head to know that the man who'd monopolized her every waking thought for the past week was riding next to her.

"Brannigan," she said with a brief nod, but didn't look at him.

They rode the circumference of the arena side by side in silence. All the way around the stadium, the only thing Ellie could think about was the way she'd been dressed when he'd burst into her camper. *Or wasn't dressed,* she corrected. She could only thank her lucky stars she'd been wearing *something.*

But the more she thought about it, the more she wished her chaste undergarments had been a little more on the feminine side. A little satin, a little lace— sexy—and none of the virginal white cotton she was accustomed to wearing. Not that a man was likely to see them. Then again, odd things did happen. She had proof of that.

Taking a deep breath, she ventured a glance at the cowboy beside her. The air lodged in her lungs. Shoulders as wide as his should be outlawed. And why hadn't she noticed how straight his nose was or his thick, black lashes? Because she'd been trying her darnedest not to, that's why.

The anger she'd felt at his high-handedness in her trailer began to melt like ice cream on an August day. She didn't care for his bossy ways, so like all the cowboys she'd ever known. But none of them ever had eyes that darkened when they looked at her. And none of them had made her ache with the need to be held in their arms.

She couldn't allow herself these feelings or let him know she had them. Still, she owed Chace Brannigan common courtesy at the very least, instead of ordering him from her rolling home. He'd saved her from having to deal with a snake that had scared her out of her scattered wits. He'd pointed out her untrustworthy lock and reminded her of the danger of not securing the new one. In less than a week he'd come to her aid more times than anyone had in her lifetime. She could afford to be more civil. Even friendly. That's all he'd asked.

The parade of participants made its way out of the arena gate. As far as Ellie knew, Chace had forgotten she was beside him. He hadn't said a word for several minutes.

"I'm sorry I was so rude today," she offered with sincerity.

He rode past her without looking her way. "Forget it."

She'd have been relieved, if it weren't for the way his mouth turned down at the corners. He was angry, and it perturbed her, considering she'd apologized. He'd never bothered to do the same. Maybe he needed a reminder.

Staring at his broad, stiff back, she lifted her chin. "Of course, I'm not the only one who forgot her manners."

They'd reached the area outside the arena and came to a halt away from the other contestants. Chace jerked around in his saddle to stare at her. "You starting on that again?"

Her heart sank and her anger rose. "I wasn't the one who came busting into someone's *home* while she was half-naked," she pointed out, and then realized what she'd just said. But when his eyes blazed to life at the mention of her state of undress, she forced herself not to look away.

His eyes darkened to deep-blue. "I'm trying to decide whether to let that remark slide on by or..."

"Or what?" she dared to ask.

He hesitated, then shook his head. "Can we have a conversation without needing boxing gloves?"

Relieved, she gave him a tentative nod. "I'd like that. If you think it's possible." And if he'd only smile. Just a little.

His gaze slid over her, hot and sexy, before he answered. "Tell you what. My ride's coming up soon. We'll call a truce and see if it lasts until then."

She nodded again, offering a weak smile as the arena announcer asked the crowd to stand for the inspirational piece and the national anthem. This was where her mind usually drifted ahead to her ride, mentally taking each barrel, feeling each movement of Sky Dancer beneath her. But tonight she couldn't even focus on that because of the man beside her. Her entire body was on alert. The scent of rodeo—hay, livestock, dust—was sharper, the air clearer, and each sound a little crisper.

When the ceremony ended, Chace cleared his throat. "Where'd you compete before Iowa?"

"Memphis. You?"

"Mesquite."

It was pretty clear he was trying to keep the conversation as generic and friendly as possible. Ellie smiled to herself, determined to follow his lead. "I considered Mesquite, but I was there earlier this year and wanted to try someplace new."

He agreed and told her about his own season. At first strained, the conversation took a friendly turn, and they both relaxed. They shared stories like old friends, leaving them both laughing. Before she knew it, their time came to an end.

"There's my call," Chace said, dismounting at the announcement of his name. "Can I trust you to keep an eye on Redneck?"

Before she had a chance to answer, he handed her the reins and turned to leave.

"Chace?"

When he stopped to look at her over his shoulder, she crooked her finger at him.

Puzzlement in his eyes, he walked back to stand beside her horse. "Something wrong?"

"A little closer," she said with a grin. When he took another step that brought him against her leg, she leaned down and ducked under his hat to plant a kiss on his cheek. "Good luck. I'll be cheering for you."

He stared at her for a moment, then, sliding his hand up her leg, he rested it on her thigh. "That oughta do it."

Unable to break his hypnotic gaze, she felt the hitch in her breath. But instead of the kiss she anticipated, he dropped his hand and turned to walk to the area behind the chutes.

"You dummy," she scolded herself, when she'd let out the breath she'd been holding. Everything had been going fine, and she'd had to go and spoil it with a simple good-luck kiss. What must he think of her now?

Chace couldn't remember a more uncomfortable bronc ride. The feel of Ellie's lips on his cheek and her soft scent had brought his body to a state of complete arousal. Nothing like that had happened to him before. But the discomfort and pain were worth a ride from hell after seeing the look in her eyes when she'd wished him luck. It must have brought him some. In spite of the state he'd been in, he was sitting in first place.

He'd gotten more than his share of good-luck kisses—among other things—during the eighteen years he'd been rodeoing. There'd even been a time or two he'd found lingerie tucked into his saddle by an overzealous buckle bunny. But nothing had ever affected him the way Ellie's gentle kiss had. Soft. Sweet. And sexy as hell. He wouldn't forget it.

But he would forget it. In time. The season would end, and they'd go their separate ways. They might meet up in Vegas, but that would be the end of it. That's the way it was supposed to be. A woman was an expense, both financially and psychologically, that he couldn't afford.

Ray met up with him on the way to his pickup to discuss the upcoming team roping event. Given the choice, Chace would have chosen to spend the time in Ellie's company, but he knew he'd be better off staying away from her. He couldn't let her or her presence interfere with his competing. He didn't want to let Ray down. Later, when the rodeo was finished for the night, maybe he'd find her, and they could discuss lucky charms. The thought brought a smile to his lips. Until he remembered she'd be meeting Jimmy Bob.

He choked on the thought.

"What'd you say?" Ray asked him.

"Nothin'." Chace kept walking, determined to put as much distance as possible between himself and Ellie. Was he nuts? He shouldn't care. But he didn't like the feeling that hit him when he thought about Ellie being anywhere near his former neighbor. As much as he didn't want to admit it, that feeling had more to do with Ellie herself than with what Jimmy Bob was up to.

"Sounded like some kinda growl," Ray said.

"You're hearing things."

"You ropin' without a horse tonight, Chace?"

Chace stopped, swearing under his breath. "I left him with Ellie."

"Want me to get him for ya?"

"Nope." Chace turned on his heel and headed back to where he'd left Ellie with his horse. It irritated him no end to think they'd had a good time together while she planned to meet another man later. A man who made him want to chew horseshoes. He knew he was being irrational. He didn't need to get tangled up with the woman. But he'd gone and spent a good half hour with her. Even worse, he'd enjoyed every second of it.

He found her still holding Redneck's reins and talking to Jimmy Bob. His first impulse was to ignore the man and haul her off her horse to give her a kiss that would set her on fire. Reason and common sense caused him to dump the idea. Jimmy Bob would take it as an invitation to start trouble.

Without a glance at the man he considered the world's biggest weasel, Chace approached the pair and took the reins from Ellie's hand. "Much obliged."

She looked down at him, surprise and what he hoped might be disappointment at his cool tone in her eyes. "Good ride."

He shrugged, but locked his gaze with hers. "Guess I'd better wish you luck now. Ray and I rope next, and we need to loosen up."

"Good luck, Chace. And to Ray, too." She broke

the gaze to glance at Jimmy Bob, then looked back at Chace. The deep breath she took caused the silky fringe on her shirt to quiver. "I'll see you at Reba's tomorrow, won't I?"

"Nothin' could keep me away," he promised, keeping his voice low and only for her ears. The grin he gave her was a poor substitute for the kiss he'd considered, but it would have to do.

He walked away without a backward glance, feeling better than he had since the first time he'd seen them together.

"I wasn't aware that you knew Chace Brannigan," he heard Jimmy Bob say.

"We're good friends," she replied. "How do *you* know him?"

Chace didn't wait to hear the answer. Jimmy Bob would come up with something untrue but believable. Jimmy Bob would know he knew Ellie and would give conning her a second thought. But knowing him, Chace felt certain that second thoughts wouldn't stop Jimmy Bob Staton. And Jimmy Bob wouldn't stop Chace.

"I wasn't sure if you'd come," Reba said when she opened the trailer door at Ellie's knock.

Ellie carried in the chocolate cake she'd baked earlier that morning and set it on the table. "Why wouldn't I?"

"Chace'll be here." Reba's eyes twinkled with mischief as she joined Ellie at the table and looked at the cake.

Ellie was too busy calming the butterflies in her stomach to reply. She'd been tempted not to show up for this lunch. Chace hadn't said anything in particular to make her feel that way. In fact, since they'd called a truce, he'd been nice. Too nice. She liked it better when he said something that riled her. Dealing with anger sure beat dealing with the other feelings he stirred in her. Like the fluttering in her middle, for instance. And he wasn't even in the vicinity!

But that was nothing compared to the way she felt when he looked at her. He'd called her beautiful, and that, she knew, wasn't true. Pretty she could work on.

"Reba?"

Busy placing plates on the table, she didn't look up. "Yeah?"

"You're about the closest thing I have to a mother."

Reba set the last plate down and moved to slip an arm around her. "That's mighty sweet of you to say. I promised your mama when you first started riding the circuit that I'd keep an eye on you."

Ellie fought off the memories caused by her friend's comment and glanced at the clock on the counter, knowing she didn't have much time. She took a heaping bowl of mashed potatoes from the counter and set them on the table. "I could use a little advice."

Reba raised an eyebrow as she sat at the table and pointed to the spot across from her. "Man problems?"

Ellie slid into the seat. Time was running out. Chace could arrive any minute, and she didn't want him hearing this. "Yes...and no. I have a dinner date tonight, and I don't have a dress to my name. I can't remember the last time I wore one. Probably at the funeral, and that was almost nine years ago."

Excitement glowed in Reba's eyes, and her smile stretched wide. "Now, that's the best news I've heard in a long time. Not about the dress, o'course. You goin' shoppin'? There's that big mall in town. I could go along and help.''

Ellie relaxed with a sigh and a grateful smile. ''That would be perfect. I don't have a clue what to look for.''

Nodding, Reba stood and grabbed a bowl of string beans. ''Let's get these vittles on the table. Chace will be here—'' She stopped and handed the bowl to Ellie. ''I plum forgot I need to get Nate,'' she said with a sigh as she untied the print apron she wore around her waist. ''If you'll just finish settin' the table, I'll go tell him we're ready to eat. Won't take but a couple of minutes.''

Before Ellie could reply, Reba was out of the trailer with a wave of her hand. Ellie wasn't sure what to do. Chace *would* be there any minute.

Hurrying to finish the chore Reba had assigned her, she silently prayed that her friend would be back before Chace arrived. The last thing she wanted was to be left alone with him.

When she heard a knock on the door, the butterflies that had calmed in her stomach suddenly took off like a fleet of jet planes. She swallowed her panic and went to open the door.

Chace stood on the trailer steps, hat in hand. ''I know I'm early, but I swear I could smell Reba's cooking clear across the lot.''

Ellie took a deep breath to steady herself. The clean, sharp scent of soap, outdoors and male nearly made her stumble when she moved back to allow him into the trailer. He'd obviously spent some time cleaning up for their little lunch. His still-damp hair gleamed, and his shirt was crisply pressed. He didn't look like a cowboy who'd been on the road for months.

"Reba will be back in a minute with Nate," she blurted out, not knowing what else to say. She looked down to see him turning his hat in his hands and recognized the nervous gesture. It calmed her enough to remember her manners. "Go ahead and sit down. I'll get us something to drink. Do you want a beer?" she asked, hurrying to the small refrigerator to escape him.

He stood by the table, shifting from one foot to the other. "Whatever you're having."

She took four glasses from the cupboard and began to fill them with ice. Her hands shook so badly, more ice went on the countertop than in the glasses, but she finally managed to get them filled. Aggravated that his presence bothered her so much, she jerked the full pitcher of tea from the refrigerator, spilling it on her shirt. Biting back a self-inflicted curse, she hefted the heavy pitcher over the first glass, missing the rim and slopping tea on the counter.

"Let me." Chace's deep voice rumbled in her ear.

She nearly dropped the pitcher in her haste to move away from him. When she bumped into the edge of the refrigerator, she came to a teetering halt. "It's heavier than I thought," she lied.

He handed her a full glass of tea, steadying her with his other hand. "You take this one. I'll bring the others."

She made the mistake of glancing up at him. The same hungry eyes she'd seen last night when he'd wished her good luck gazed down into hers. She'd watched him and his partner team rope to take first place in the standings and had half expected him to come over and congratulate her on doing the same in her own event. But she hadn't seen him again until much later when she was leaving with J.R., and that had been from a distance. Chace had sat on his horse looking like the loneliest cowboy she'd ever seen. If it hadn't been for J.R. demanding her attention, she'd have gone over to Chace in an instant.

Ellie took the glass to the table and slid onto the seat. Chace followed, taking his place beside her, and she moved as far to her right as she could, away from him.

Silence bounced off the walls of the trailer until Chace broke it. "Where did you meet your friend?"

"My friend?" Ellie asked. "Oh, you mean J.R. He's my agent."

"Agent?"

She nodded, wishing Reba would hurry. "He's helping me sell my ranch."

His mouth pulled down in a frown. "You have a ranch?"

"Well, it isn't only mine. It belongs to my brothers and me. Matt's twenty-four and Brett is twenty-one. They've been working it on their own for about six years, since I started riding the circuit full-time," she explained.

Chace studied her. "They don't like ranching?"

"It isn't that, it's—"

Reba burst through the door, saving Ellie from having to explain herself to Chace.

"Sorry to run out on you two. Nate'll be here shortly." Reba settled at the table, picked up a fork and smiled at them. "So where are you two goin' to dinner tonight?"

Ellie felt Chace stiffen beside her. She could have kicked herself for not telling Reba that her date was with J.R., but she'd known how Reba would have reacted. She sneaked a glance at Chace.

He gave Reba a strained smile. "Didn't know we were."

Reba's eyes, wide with surprise, narrowed, and she gave a loud sniff before pinning Ellie with a disgusted glint in her eyes. "Guess you can go shoppin' by yourself."

Chapter Four

Now that Chace had an idea of what Jimmy Bob was up to, he had to find a way to put a stop to it. As badly as he wanted to catch the weasel in the act, he couldn't let this sale of Ellie's go through. Not if J.R. was involved.

But there was more to it than a simple sale of property. He could feel it in his bones. Why did Ellie want to sell her ranch? Did the brothers she'd mentioned want to sell? Were they in some kind of financial trouble, about to lose it?

He shook his head. He didn't have any answers. Ellie wasn't willing to discuss the details with him. Somehow he needed to get some answers.

Mounting his horse, he was determined to do just that. He'd already seen how she reacted to the slightest suggestion. If he was going to help her and get the drop on J.R., too, he couldn't let her know what he was up to. If he could get her to trust him, maybe then he could get her to talk to him.

For the life of him he didn't know why he was getting involved. He had his own problems. But he couldn't stand by and not do anything. He'd never forgive himself if anything happened to her. He was in it for the long haul now.

And he'd have to do it without it interfering with his own competing. Keeping an eye on the little barrel racer hadn't bothered his riding yet. Still, he needed to keep his mind on his competition. He couldn't afford to let preoccupation with her or her troubles affect his riding or roping. Finals and the Triple B had to come first.

From a short distance he saw Ellie pull her pickup into an empty space. Maybe now was the time to start finding out what she had in mind as far as J.R. was concerned.

By the time she climbed out of her truck, he was rounding the back of her camper on horseback, and he greeted her.

She let out a yelp and dropped three of the packages she was carrying. "Thanks a lot, Brannigan."

"What'd you do? Buy out the store?" He slid to the ground and looped the reins on a nearby pickup, while she bent to retrieve her bundles. Stooping to lend a hand, he couldn't help but notice what she was so quickly scooping into the sacks. Bits of lace and satin caught his attention. He picked up one wisp of lace that remotely resembled a pair of woman's panties and held it up. "What's this?"

She snatched it from him, her face red. "Go play Boy Scout somewhere else, will you? I can pick up my own things."

"These are yours?"

"Wipe that grin off your face," she snapped, kneeling to gather the spilled garments.

If she'd bothered to look at him, she'd have seen that he wasn't smiling. He could barely take his eyes off the pile of sexy underthings. Imagining her in them had his head spinning and his body responding. He bit back a groan. What the hell was she planning with J.R.?

"That's some bag of goodies you have there," he finally said when he had his voice under control. "Doesn't look like the Ellie I know."

After cramming everything back into the bags, she got to her feet but didn't look at him. "A girl can change her mind, can't she?"

About as often as she changed her underwear, he thought with disgust, his unease growing. Climbing back in the saddle before his mouth got him in trouble, he turned his horse to leave. "I gotta go get some practice in with Ray. I'll see you in the arena."

She held the bundles close to her chest and met his gaze, her cheeks still pink. "Yeah, I have things to do, too."

He quickly bade her goodbye and rode away, his irritation growing. J.R. had always been too bright for his own good. He'd been a sneak as a kid and worse as a man. But Chace would put a stop to this business with Ellie. Jimmy Bob Staton wasn't about to get a glimpse of the things she'd stuffed in that sack. Not if Chace had his way about it.

On his way back to his truck he spied Reba outside her trailer. She knew Ellie better than anybody. Maybe she could give him a clue about what was going on.

"You talk to Ellie?" she asked as he dismounted and tied his horse to the step railing.

"What's going on, Reba? Why is she selling her ranch? She need the money?"

"Far as I know, the place is doin' okay. But she hates it. Her folks—" Reba clamped her mouth shut and shook her head, sending her carroty curls bouncing. "Let's just say there's personal reasons why she doesn't want it."

Knowing Reba as he did, Chace didn't bother to dig any deeper. The woman might love knowing everybody's business, but she'd keep it all close if she thought sharing would cause any harm. He'd have to get the story from Ellie, one way or another.

"I'll keep an eye on her," he promised. He wasn't going to let her get hurt, and if that meant following her, he would. "I don't think she remembers mentioning the name of the place they were going to tonight."

She pinned him with a knowing look, a gleam in her eye. "If you see any hanky-panky goin' on, you put a stop to it, you hear?"

He didn't want to think about Ellie and J.R. getting cozy. Just the thought made his stomach roll. "He's after the ranch, not Ellie."

"You think so? I wouldn't put nothin' past him. And what with her havin' her mind set on settlin' down in the city like him, nothin' would surprise me."

Her words caught him off guard. When she started to walk away, he reached for her arm and turned her back around to face him. "What do you mean by settling down in the city?"

"Did you think this was just about her ranch?" Reba asked, her eyes wide. "That's just the tip of the iceberg. Ellie has this foolish notion that she wants to quit rodeo and move to the city."

"That's crazy." But realization at what she was getting at stopped him cold. Ellie Warren, with or without the ranch, was a prize any man would be a fool to turn down.

Reba stepped closer and poked his chest with her finger. "What about you, Brannigan?"

He squirmed under her intense stare. "Me?"

"Are you in love with her?"

"Nope," he said with certainty and backed up a step. "She's a mighty fine little package, but other than not wanting to see anybody take advantage of her, I don't have any designs on her."

"That's too bad," Reba answered with a smile he didn't care for. "This bein' your last year and all, I'd a thought you might be ready to settle down. With somebody like Ellie, o'course. You both have ranchin' and rodeo backgrounds."

"You can stop your matchmaking, Reba. I'm not looking to get hitched to anybody."

"No man ever is," she said as he turned to walk away. "'Specially a cowboy."

He pulled his hat off and raked his hand through his hair. He knew what she was getting at, but she didn't understand his situation. He had responsibilities now. From his brother Trey's last report, the Triple B needed more than just the money a double championship would provide. It was time to quit rodeo and go back to the ranch to help get it running in top gear again—as a cattle ranch, not a dude ranch. Marrying Ellie, or anyone else, was the last thing on his mind.

But, he admitted to himself with disgust, Ellie was the first thing on his mind. And not just because of J.R.

He jammed his hat on his head. "Nothing's going

to happen to her.'' But he wasn't comfortable with the idea of spying on her.

With one foot in the stirrup, ready to mount again after her race, Ellie heard her name called. She stopped, afraid to look over her shoulder, and tried to calm her racing heart. The voice was too familiar, and she didn't want to face Chace right now.

"I'm kind of in a hurry," she told him, and started to swing her other leg up.

"I won't slow you down." He gripped her calf, sending a flash of heat through her, and moved her leg back to the ground. Taking the reins, he placed a hand at her back and moved her along. "You did great tonight."

She glanced at him and shook her head as they walked away. "I took second," she answered with a sigh.

"Doesn't mean you didn't do great."

She looked up to see his smile. In spite of her disappointment in her ride, she couldn't stop the ribbon of heat uncurling in her. Ignoring it, she pointed at the buckles in his hand. "But you took first in both events."

He shrugged. "Everybody has good rodeos and bad. You'll do better next time. Maybe I won't."

"It's not the same for you," she argued. "You're a three-time bronc champ. There's no question you'll go to Finals this year."

"Can't count on anything, hon. Accidents happen." His hand slid from the middle of her back to settle around her waist. "Nothing's for certain. You ought to know that."

"All I know is that I have to make Finals this year.

And if I don't win the next three rodeos, I won't.'' He was right. Anything could happen. But she couldn't think about that. As it was, she was having trouble thinking with his arm snugged around her. It was all she could do not to give in to the need to lean her head against him.

He pulled her even closer. ''I've got my money on you making it.''

His faith in her gave her a warm glow. Even her brothers, who cheered her from the ranch, had never made her feel so good. It wasn't only his words that brought a flush of warmth to her face. Heat infused her whole body. She knew she ought to pull away, but she couldn't do it.

''Why don't I put Sky Dancer up for you?''

His offer surprised her. He knew she had a date with J.R., and from his reaction at lunch, she hadn't thought it pleased him much. Maybe she'd been wrong. Maybe she'd only imagined he might be interested in her. The thought left her feeling flat. Even with his arm around her, she couldn't be sure he was being anything more than friendly.

''That's real nice of you, Chace.''

She expected him to say good-night and lead Sky Dancer away, but he stayed with her until they reached her camper. At her door he used one hand to tie the reins he held to a handle. With the other, he turned her toward him and slowly pulled her against him.

Ripples of electricity shot through her, and her heart hammered in a wild rhythm.

''I know you're in a rush,'' he said, his voice husky.

''Y-yes,'' she stammered, her own voice a whisper. ''J.R. will be here any minute and I need to change—''

His mouth came down on hers, stealing what little breath she had left. A tiny portion of her mind told her she should pull back and put an end to this sudden assault on her senses, but her lips seemed to have a mind of their own. Her body, too, as she stood on tiptoe, her arms slipping up and around his neck of their own accord. She heard and felt his groan, while everything around them disappeared, except the taste and feel of the man who held her in his arms.

When his tongue touched her lips, a tremor of heat went through her. Her gasp of surprise opened her to his exploration, and she responded with her own moan of need. He wrapped her tightly in his arms, bringing her higher and closer, and her feet left the ground. Her body turned to molten lava as she pressed herself to him, feeling his heat match her own.

She thought she'd died and gone to heaven, but when his lips left hers and he kissed his way down her throat, she knew she hadn't found paradise. Not with the flames building to a bonfire inside her.

Before she had a chance to think about what was happening to her body, he stole her mouth again in a second mind-blowing kiss, and she instinctively answered his passion with hers. She forgot where she was, until he ended the kiss and set her on the step leading to her camper. Gasping for breath on legs that threatened to buckle, she clung to his arms to keep from crumpling into a heap.

With one finger he tilted her chin up to gaze into her eyes. "You have a good dinner, Ellie."

Picking up her hat, which had fallen to the ground, he handed it to her, then left her standing there, breathless and tingling, after planting one lingering kiss on her lips.

"Oh, mercy." She sighed, touching her fingertips to her bereft lips and grabbing the handle of the door to steady herself. How would she ever get through dinner with that on her mind?

The minute Chace saw Ellie leave the table in the fancy restaurant, he started moving toward the door. The last thing he wanted was to get caught. But the place was packed, and the maître d' had been giving him the eye since he'd refused a table nearly an hour earlier. After a quick look again in Ellie's direction, he left his manners behind him and pushed his way through the waiting patrons.

He didn't stop until his feet hit the pavement outside the restaurant. She had seen him. Looking over his shoulder, he hoped she hadn't recognized him. That's all the bundle of dynamite would need to set her off. Certain the people moving aside were making way for a fireball headed in his direction, he fought down the panic that rose in this throat. He'd rather take on the world's meanest bronc than face Ellie at that moment.

To his right he noticed a group of women huddled together. Without thinking of the consequences, he reached into his pocket and pulled out his money clip. A quick look at the crowd—where the top of burnished golden hair could now be seen—had him ripping a fifty-dollar bill from the wad in his hand. He moved next to the closest of the young women and slipped an arm around her waist, while he pressed the money into her hand.

"Pretend you're my date," he whispered to her. With his most dazzling smile, he quickly eased her away from the others, who'd stopped chattering and stood gaping at him.

Before he could say more, he heard his name being called from behind him. He turned his head to see Ellie bulldozing her way out of the crowd.

The woman in his grasp took a step back, pulling away from him. "Is...is that your wife?"

A glance at her terrified expression almost convinced him to release her, but Ellie was approaching, and he realized he'd rather have a hysterical stranger on his hands than have to answer to Ellie for being there alone.

"No," he assured the brunette, holding tight. "Just a friend. You don't have to say anything. Just smile."

She stared at him for a second before complying as Ellie came to a stop in front of them.

Ellie looked from him to the woman, comprehension clear in her eyes. "Oh. I'm sorry, Chace. I didn't know— I guess you're...with someone."

"Hey, Ellie. I thought I saw you inside." He said a silent thank-you to the powers that be and smiled down at the almost speechless Ellie. Sweat beaded on his forehead, but he kept smiling. He might as well be in hell, he figured. He'd sure be headed that way after this little scene.

To his surprise, the brunette offered her hand to Ellie. "Hi, I'm Julie."

Ellie blinked, then took the woman's hand, offering an embarrassed and apologetic smile that included Chace. "Ellie Warren. Chace and I are friends. From the rodeo," she hurried to add. "I really am sorry for interrupting your evening. It's just that I thought— Well, I thought he was checking up on me and my date."

Julie turned her gaze to Chace. "Really?"

He couldn't ignore the reproach in the woman's

eyes and eased away from her. "I'll be right back. Will you be okay for a minute?"

The look she gave him was enough to cement his belief in the sisterhood of women. He needed to get Ellie away as fast as possible before the whole thing blew up in his face. If Ellie got a hint at what he'd done, he'd likely be stuck between two wildcats.

Taking Ellie by the elbow, he turned her toward the restaurant. "Let me take you back inside."

"I truly am sorry, Chace," she said as he made a pathway for both of them through the waiting patrons.

"Don't worry about it. You couldn't have known." Damn right, he thought to himself, since even he hadn't known the woman five minutes earlier.

"I hope she's not upset," Ellie said, looking up at him.

His chest tightened and he had to swallow the knot of guilt in his throat. "Naw, she's a good sport."

"She's beautiful."

He heard the soft hitch in her voice and felt like a bigger weasel than J.R. The pink of her cheeks and shimmer in her eyes nearly killed him on the spot. He hadn't set out to hurt her, but he had. Hell, he was trying to save her.

"Yeah? I hadn't noticed," he finally answered. It struck him as funny that it was the first truthful thing he'd said to her that evening.

Hoping to avoid J.R., he met with disappointment when her date appeared. He released her with reluctance and greeted his former neighbor. "Evenin', J.R."

She looked up at Chace, missing the warning in J.R.'s eyes. "I hope you both enjoy the rest of your evening."

Chace avoided J.R.'s scowl and shrugged. "We were ready to call it a night."

She turned back to J.R. "I'm sorry about keeping you waiting. I...um, ran into Chace, and he introduced his date."

"His date?"

Chace had to grit his teeth to keep from wiping the satisfied smile off J.R.'s face. "Yeah, well, I'd better get back to...Janice."

Nodding in the direction of J.R., Chace gave Ellie a smile he didn't feel and touched his finger to the brim of his hat. The thought of leaving her with J.R. made his head ache.

Outside again, he kneaded the back of his neck and wondered about the quizzical look Ellie had given him before he'd walked away. Reba would probably rake him over the coals for pulling the stunt he had, but it couldn't be helped. If Ellie found out he was there alone—

A tug on his jacket sleeve caught his attention.

"Take your money, cowboy," the brunette said, stuffing the bill he'd given her into his jacket pocket. "I've heard about you rodeo Romeos. I hope you get everything you deserve from that sweet woman, you sneak."

He stared at her retreating back. *Women!* Who could figure them? He wished he could. Especially Ellie. There was no telling how she would react when he warned her about J.R. And he would. First thing in the morning.

Ellie closed the trailer door behind Sky Dancer before circling around to lock her camper door. She hadn't slept well. Dreams of Chace's kisses brought her awake more often than she cared to think. Each time she reminded herself that he'd followed her, but it didn't stop the steamy visions that had left her breathless and sleepless.

After checking the trailer hitch, she slammed the cover on it. She hoped Chace was suffering from indigestion. He deserved no better. She didn't want to see him again, but of all the bad luck, they were headed for the same rodeo. She'd compete somewhere else if she hadn't already sent her entry money, but she couldn't afford to change plans now.

Double checking the camper door, she spun around, ready to get a start on the drive. Her heart sank when she looked up to see Chace walking her way. Her luck was running bad.

"Mornin', Ellie."

Taking a deep breath, she planted her hands on her hips and glared at him. "That was a real slimy thing you did last night, Brannigan."

His devilish grin was bone melting. "If you're referring to our kiss—"

"I'm referring to the fact that you followed me last night. I don't even remember kissing you." The lie sprang readily to her lips. She'd practiced it half the night. That kiss had burned its way into her soul and was fully entrenched in her memory, no matter what else he'd done since.

He strolled toward her, his gait easy and confident. "I don't know what you're talking about."

"Are you going to tell me you weren't alone last night? You forgot her name was Julie, not Janice. And we were right behind you when you left. I saw what happened, and I heard what your *date* said. It didn't take me long to figure out what was going on. You followed me.''

His grin didn't falter. ''Now, would I do that to you?''

''In a heartbeat.''

She tried to push past him to get to her truck, but he stopped her, his hands gripping her shoulders. ''Somebody needs to warn you about J. R. Staton.''

She looked up to see his blue eyes turned hard and steely. ''And I suppose that's why you're here so bright and early this morning. Forget it, Brannigan. I'll see who I want to see.''

Studying her, his eyes softened, and he touched a finger to her cheek. ''Is that why you have dark circles under your eyes?''

His touch did more to her than a brush fire did to dry rangeland. It was all she could do not to beg him to hold her. But she didn't. She couldn't give in to her body's urgings. She was stronger than that. She had to be.

She took a step back. ''It has nothing to do with you.''

''I'm going to worry about you all the way to Austin, Ellie,'' he said in a soft, warm voice, and moved closer to her.

Her heart pounded, and the words she needed to say stuck in her throat. ''W-well…don't. I'll be…fine.''

In an instant he had her backed up against her camper. With his hands planted on either side of her head, and his body mere inches from hers, she was trapped. She bit the inside of her cheek to check the groan that threatened to give her away. She wanted him to touch her. To kiss her again. It took all of her concentration to keep from giving in.

Afraid to even glance at him, she kept her head lowered. "Do me a favor, will you?"

"Name it."

The warmth of his voice made her knees weak, but she took a deep breath and forced herself to look up at him, willing her heart to be still and her voice to remain cool. "When we get to Austin, pretend you don't know me."

He moved one hand to place it over his heart and gave his head a sad shake. "You've really wounded me, hon. I can't do that."

"Then stop telling me how to run my life."

He hesitated before stepping back, then he reached into his shirt pocket and pulled out a card. Taking her hand, he pressed the paper into it. "This is my cell phone number. If you need me—or want me—for anything, you call me, you hear?"

Frustrated by her inability to resist him and his obvious refusal to listen to her, she crumpled the card and dropped it on the ground at his feet. "You just don't get it, do you?"

He bent down and picked up the card. Slipping his arm around her waist and pulling her close, he stuffed it in the back pocket of her jeans. "Admit it, hon. I do things to you that J. R. Staton only wished he could do."

She opened her mouth to tell him exactly what she thought of his egotism, but before she could get a word out, he'd taken possession of her lips. Her argument was gone on the breeze.

Chapter Five

"Not now," Ellie groaned.

Poised on the front bumper of her pickup, she stood peering into the labyrinth of her engine. Why hadn't she listened to Matt when he'd tried to teach her basic engine repair? If she had, maybe she would have a clue why her truck had suddenly died out here in the middle of nowhere.

"Some independent woman you are, Ellie Warren," she muttered as she climbed down. The urge to kick the bumper was strong, but she controlled her temper.

This was going to cost her some time. A lot of time, by the look of it. Even though she was on the Interstate, she'd seen little traffic since leaving Tuscon behind. By her calculations, she was somewhere in New Mexico, and although the scenery was beautiful, she was far from help.

With nothing to do but wait until someone stopped, she checked on Sky Dancer. If it hadn't been for the shoe he'd thrown, she would saddle and ride him to the nearest town. She'd calculated her drive so she could see some sights and still arrive a day early in Austin to have him shod. If help came soon, and the trouble with her truck wasn't major, she could still do that.

Latching the gate behind her horse, she heard a vehicle behind at a distance and turned to see a truck coming over the top of the hill. Silhouetted against the mountains in the background, the truck drew nearer—near enough to recognize the bright blue stretch-cab. The last person she wanted to see was Chace Brannigan, but as the truck came to a slow halt behind her rig, she was reminded that luck was rarely on her side when it came to him.

"Hi, Ray," she called to Chace's roping partner, who exited the cab first once they'd stopped.

"Looks like you're havin' some trouble there, girl." He pushed back his hat with the finger of a bandaged hand and waited for Chace to alight from the truck.

When Chace climbed out, he looked Ellie up and down. Shaking his head slowly, he approached her. "Mornin', ma'am," he said, touching the brim of his hat.

Ma'am? She stared at him, speechless.

"You seem to have a problem," he went on, while she continued to stare at him. "Where are you headed?"

Unable to believe what she was hearing, she planted her hands on her hips and glared at him. "You know darned well where I'm headed, Chace Brannigan. The same place you are."

He ducked his head and toed the dirt on the side of the highway, but not before she saw him fighting a smile. When he looked at her again, there was no mistaking the twinkle in his eyes. "I'm headed to Austin, and I don't believe we've met."

"Oh, for crying out loud," she muttered, remembering the last thing she'd said to him in Phoenix. If he was determined to hold her to her words, even in this situation, she'd play along. Especially if it meant getting back on the road. Drawing herself up, she held out her hand. "Ellie Warren. I'm headed to Austin, too."

He took her hand and placed it in the crook of his arm. "Well, Miss Warren— It *is* miss, isn't it?"

Biting her cheek to keep from laughing, she could only nod.

"Then let's take a look and see what the trouble is."

"I was just driving along and it quit," she explained as they walked together to the front of her truck.

"Sounds like a battery or an alternator." He released her and looked inside the engine. "Did you notice any of the lights on the instrument panel come on?"

"No, I didn't." She was glad he was otherwise occupied and couldn't see her embarrassment. How many times would he have to come to her rescue? And when would she admit to herself that most of those times she was glad he had?

Behind her, Ray cleared his throat. "Thought I saw somethin' layin' in the road back there."

"Alternator belt." Chace straightened and reached up to lower the hood over the engine.

"Do you have a spare?" Ellie asked, and explained her need to be in Austin a day early.

"Different belts for different vehicles," he said. "I

have the tools, but we still need a belt. Our best bet is Las Cruces, if anything else is wrong.''

''Wrong?'' Her stomach knotted at the thought of missing the rodeo. She couldn't afford not to compete. ''Like what?''

Slipping his arm around her, he steered her toward her camper. ''Nothing serious, but we'll want it checked out to make sure there's no problem with the battery or the alternator.'' He turned to his partner. ''Any suggestions?''

''Well now, I can't do no ropin' for a bit. Caught my hand in the rope back in Phoenix and gotta let it heal,'' Ray explained to Ellie with an apologetic smile. ''But I'd say the best thing to do to save time would be for you two to head on to Austin, while I take care of Miss Ellie's rig.''

Chace nodded in agreement. ''Good idea.''

She looked at Chace. ''This won't hurt your team roping standings, will it?''

His smile, as always, warmed her heart. ''If it does, we'll make up for it later. Ray and I aren't worried. Let's just concentrate on the problem at hand.''

At the rear of her camper, he lowered himself to the step and patted the empty space beside him. Ellie eyed the spot he indicated and hesitated. Only the day before she'd told him to pretend he didn't know her, and yet here he was, helping her out of a tight spot. Again.

The drive out of Phoenix had given her time to think about what she'd said to him, and she knew it had been because she was beginning to depend on him too much. He'd been right when he'd said he did things to her that J.R. never could. No man ever had, and she wondered if any man ever would again. It wasn't just the way her body responded each time he was near. It was her heart. Chace was the kind of man any woman would be a fool to turn down. But she didn't want a man. And until recently, she hadn't thought she needed one. But Chace had proven to her that she did. Not for the things he did for her, but the things he did to her and her heart.

"…and then I'll just catch up with you two in Austin sometime tomorrow," Ray was saying.

With sudden clarity Ellie realized what that meant. It wasn't just a quick trip to the next rodeo. It was a good twelve-hour drive, and it was getting late in the day. "Tomorrow?" she asked Chace.

"It'll take that much time."

She could tell by the way he watched her that he expected her to argue. This time she wouldn't. She didn't have a choice. "Okay," she said and shrugged.

"Let's not sit around, then," Chace said, getting to his feet. "While I get the number and call a tow truck, why don't you two get the horses switched?"

She was grateful to do something to keep her mind off Chace and her troubles. Sky Dancer cooperated with the switch, but Ray's roping horse wasn't as eager to step into Ellie's trailer. The more she tried to help, the worse it seemed to make the situation, so she excused herself and left it to Ray.

"Everything's taken care of," Chace told her when she neared his truck cab. "The tow truck will be here soon, and I have a good mechanic lined up in Las Cruces to check out your truck."

Worried about whether they'd drive straight through or stop somewhere for the night, Ellie answered with a nod.

"Is your horse in my trailer?"

She nodded again.

"Then let's get your stuff moved."

When he started to walk away, she touched his arm and he turned to look at her. "I don't know how to thank you."

From the spark of heat that blazed in his eyes, it was clear he had an idea of how she might go about that, but he only smiled. "Don't worry about it. I'm glad Ray and I came along and found you. Just tell me what you need to bring with you, and we'll get it done and be on the road."

She listed off the items from her trailer that she couldn't do without until Ray met them in Austin with her rig. But she didn't mention the barrel of sanity that would probably come in handy. Being that close to Chace for that long would be an experience she wasn't sure was a good idea, considering the effect he had on her.

She quickly scolded herself for not feeling the relief she should feel at knowing she would arrive safely in Austin and in plenty of time to get Sky Dancer tended to. But all she could think about was the time she'd be spending with Chace in his truck.

With her clothes and other necessities neatly stowed behind the seat in Chace's pickup, Ellie watched him carry a bale of hay from her trailer to his. He'd taken off his shirt and balanced the bale over one shoulder. Muscles bulged and rippled, and she had a hard time not staring.

"Did you remember your bell?" he asked her as she pretended to concentrate on the bucket of water she was taking to Sky Dancer.

"Bell?"

He stopped in front of her, forcing her to look at him, and grinned. "Your burglar alarm. In case I try

to—'' he bent down and placed a kiss on her ear
''—steal a kiss along the way,'' he finished, his whisper tickling and arousing at the same time.

''Chace,'' she warned, but couldn't stop her giggle.

''Ah, you *can* smile.'' His lips touched hers briefly, and then he stepped back with a cocky smile on his face. ''Now, about that bell—''

Dipping her hand in the bucket, she scooped a handful of water and flipped it at him. The next thing she knew, he'd dumped the hay and had one arm holding her tightly against him. With his other hand he took the bucket from her. ''That's no way to treat the man who rescued you, not once, but twice. Maybe you need to be taught a lesson.''

Expecting a bucket of water on her head, she was surprised when he claimed her lips with his. What started as teasing quickly turned to a declaration of need and passion. Unable to stop herself, she answered with her own desire, reaching up to wrap her arms around his neck and pull herself closer. She barely heard the bucket hit the ground. Barely noticed the water splashing up the leg of her jeans. The only thing she knew was the scent of the man who plundered her mouth and the heat of his body pressed to hers.

''Tow truck's a'comin'.''

The words found their way to Ellie's brain and she pulled away from Chace. Turning, she saw Ray's wide but embarrassed grin. Ignoring the heat inflaming her face, she headed for her camper. ''Maybe I ought to get that bell after all.''

Chace took his eyes off the road ahead long enough to steal a glance at Ellie. The little woman was as tough as they came, but if the way she'd kissed him earlier was any indication, she was having problems staying that way.

"You still mad at me?" he asked.

She turned to look at him, an inner battle evident in her eyes. "What makes you think I'm mad?"

He nearly choked on a laugh. "Could be because you've hardly said a word all afternoon." *And if you hugged the door any tighter,* he didn't add, *you'd be hanging out the window.*

"I'm used to traveling alone."

"Uh-huh." He flexed his fingers on the steering wheel, suddenly realizing how tightly he'd been gripping it. Ever since they'd left Ray to deal with towing Ellie's truck and trailer, not to mention that kiss, he'd been on edge.

Her silence bothered him. He'd only been teasing her with the kiss to get her mind off the damage done to her truck. But by the time the wrecker arrived, forcing them apart, the teasing had become something much more. It was pretty obvious that she didn't want to acknowledge that there was something going on between them. So why the hell did he keep coming back for more? Was it the challenge she presented or something else that kept him from taking to the hills like he normally would?

"When do you think we'll get into Austin?" she asked.

"Sometime tomorrow evening." Which meant they would spend one night on the road. They weren't far from El Paso, but with close to a ten-hour drive from there to Austin, they'd have to stop or drive all night. Any time he could avoid an all-nighter, he did. He wasn't sure yet how they'd handle the sleeping arrangements. He wasn't even sure he wanted to think about it.

"I hadn't planned to get there until tomorrow, anyway," she explained. "I was going to drive to San Antonio and visit some of the places I missed last year when I was there."

"You like playing tourist?" he asked, seeing a new side of Ellie.

She turned in the seat to look at him and drew her knees up close, her eyes sparkling. "I figure I might as well take every opportunity I can to see the country. It makes the traveling more fun, you know?"

Chace nodded. In all the years he'd traveled the circuit, he'd taken a little time to see the sights, too. "We Texans are pretty proud of our state. I wouldn't want you to miss the chance."

"Do you have family in Texas?"

"Two brothers, both younger." He looked at her and smiled at her surprise. "Didn't know we had that in common, did you?"

"Where are they? Are they rodeoers, too?"

"Nope. Trey—he's the youngest—is a rancher, and Dev struck out on his own not long after I did. I haven't heard anything from him for a couple of years, but he calls Trey now and then."

Her eyes lost their usual sparkle. "That's sad. Is your brother's ranch far from Austin?"

Considering that she planned to sell hers, Chace decided not to correct her about who owned the ranch. And he wasn't eager to see Trey. He and Ray had talked about stopping at the Triple B before heading into Austin. It wouldn't have been out of the way by much, but he'd vetoed the idea. Until he was sure he had his spot in Nationals tied up tight, there wasn't much to say to Trey.

"Far enough," he finally answered.

"Don't you all get along?"

Although he didn't want to get into this discussion, he felt he owed her something. "Trey and I don't always agree on some things, but other than that, we get along pretty good. And Dev's his own man. He'll show up again when he's ready."

"Parents?"

"Just us."

"Yeah, me, too." She attempted a small smile, but the crease of a frown marred it, and pain was evident in her dark eyes.

He couldn't think of a way to ease her troubles. He'd already tried it earlier with the kiss, and it hadn't turned out the way he'd hoped. In fact, it seemed to drive them even farther apart. That was something he didn't want to happen.

As they reached El Paso, the sun was beginning to set behind them. He could see that she was getting tired. Before long they'd have to stop somewhere for the night.

"Do you want to get a room?" he asked, breaking another long period of silence.

"Together?"

"Come on, Ellie. I'm not a lecher. I meant separate rooms." But had he? He couldn't deny that, in the back of his mind, he imagined them together, even though he knew it wasn't possible.

"Don't you and Ray usually sleep in the back?"

"Not when there's storms around."

She craned her neck to look out the window. "Not

a cloud in the sky, and I don't want you to have to put out the extra expense of a room for yourself.''

He suspected she didn't want to stretch her own budget. "It's not a problem. I'll spring for both rooms.''

Shaking her head, she attempted a smile. "Maybe we should just drive on through to Austin.''

That wasn't an option. Thanks to Ellie, he hadn't slept well the night before. Besides being worried about her dealings with J.R., what she'd said had wounded him. He'd spent half the night wanting to help her avoid something that could destroy her, and the other half thinking he'd be better off if he did what she'd told him to and leave her alone. He'd finally talked himself into forgetting about it so he could get some sleep.

And then he'd found her on the side of the road with her broken-down truck.

It only took Chace a second to think of another option for the sleeping arrangements. "There's plenty of room for you here in the cab. I'll sleep in the back.''

Ellie seemed to consider the suggestion. "I guess we can do that. Where will we stop?''

"There's a place between El Paso and Fort Stockton. We can stay there for the night.''

He drove for another two hours before the sun had completely set and the stars had come out. Pulling off the Interstate and into the rest area, he chose a spot where the traffic wouldn't bother them. If it had been him and Ray, they'd have stopped somewhere off the highway. Modern conveniences weren't something they cared about. But having Ellie with him made a difference.

As soon as he shut off the engine, she reached for

the door handle. "I'm really beat," she said, opening the door and stepping out of the truck. "I'll just go up to the rest room and freshen up before I turn in."

Chace scrambled from the truck and hurried to catch up with her. "I'll keep you company."

"You don't need to," she said, quickening her steps.

He gently took her arm and brought her to a halt. "Not without me. Look around, Ellie. See those semis over there? And notice how dark it is where there aren't any lights? I'd be a fool to let you walk around by yourself. Anything could happen."

"But, Chace…"

He kept hold of her and led her up the shadowed path. "Don't you read the newspaper or listen to the news? Bad things happen to people all the time. Especially women."

Her quiet laughter echoed in the open air. "They happen in broad daylight, too," she said. "Are you going to be my lifelong bodyguard?"

They'd reached the building that housed the rest rooms, and he turned her to face him. Now that she brought up the idea, he wasn't sure he'd mind keeping an eye on her. It was crazy, but he couldn't deny it. It didn't mean he wanted to make any kind of commitment or declare his undying love, but the thought of being with her for an extended period of time felt right, even though it took him by surprise.

He reached out to tug on a wisp of hair that had escaped her braid. "For this trip I'm responsible for you."

In the dim light shed by a bare yellow bulb hanging just inside the opening to the women's side of the building, he couldn't see her face clearly. The silence surrounded them, and he could have sworn he heard her heart beating. Or was that his own, racing in his ears? She was so close, so soft, so sweet. But she was also vulnerable. A woman alone.

"I'll wait right here for you," he said, taking a step back and putting some distance between them.

"I'll be fine." She turned and walked away, but stopped before she entered the building and looked back. "Thanks."

"Anytime."

When she disappeared, he let out the breath he hadn't known he'd been holding. Being around Ellie was almost more than he could take. But at the same time, he hadn't found a way to stay away from her. If he knew she might be around, he found himself seeking her out. He thought about her more often than he cared to admit. And that wasn't normal. Not for him, anyway.

They had a lot in common, and he realized that he liked her more than he ever imagined he could like a woman. He genuinely enjoyed being in her company. He liked teasing her, talking to her and listening to what she had to say. He even liked worrying about her, in spite of knowing he shouldn't.

And he liked kissing her. Damn, he really liked that.

"All done," she said, coming out into the open again.

Slipping an arm around her shoulder, he noticed that she'd released her braid. A soft, sweet scent drifted through the night air, and he pulled her close and started down the path toward his truck. Yeah, he sure did like kissing her, and he'd probably like even more.

"Are you sure you'll be all right in there?" he asked as they reached his truck.

"It isn't my camper, but I've slept in worse places."

She reached for the door, but he caught her hand and held it. "There's always the back of the truck," he dared to suggest.

For a moment she hesitated, then she looked up at the black sky dotted with millions of stars. "Doesn't it get cold at night in this part of Texas?"

He pressed her hand to his chest and drew her close. This time he not only heard but he felt her heart racing, and he smiled to himself. There was something happening, all right. No matter what she might say to make him think otherwise.

"Chace," she said on a whispered breath.

It sounded like a plea, but not a plea for release. In an instant he had her in his arms. As he kissed her sweet lips, she pressed herself to him, the heat from their bodies mingling to become one flame that threatened to consume them. He explored her mouth with his tongue as his hands explored her body, smoothing over every soft curve. Cupping her bottom with both hands, he lifted her higher and tighter, then pressed her against the side of the truck. She wound her arms around his neck and answered every thrust of his tongue with one of her own. Sensations like he'd never known overtook him. He longed to make this more than an embrace, more than a kiss.

He swept her into his arms, his lips never leaving hers. It would be so simple to—

No. This was Ellie, the woman who infuriated and inflamed him at the same time. Sweet, stubborn Ellie. Not someone who would enjoy a brief fling. And he wasn't the type who wanted anything more than that.

If she were any other woman, he wouldn't stop, knowing persuasion often won out. But she was Ellie.

With one hand he opened the passenger door and moved to place her on the seat. It was torture to break the kiss, and when he did, her arms stayed around his neck. Easing away from her, he took her hands in his. "If you need anything, let me know."

A soft sigh escaped her kiss-swollen lips. Wisps of hair curled to frame her face, and he lifted them away. Her gaze sought his and he attempted a smile.

"Chace?"

This wasn't the time. This wasn't the woman, even though he desperately wanted her to be. But a woman was an expense he couldn't afford. Even one as simple and sweet as Ellie. After what Reba had told him, he knew Ellie wasn't looking for a rodeoer. She needed someone who was stable and could give her the kind of home she wanted. Even though he didn't plan to compete much longer, he suspected she wasn't crazy about cowboys of any kind. And that was something he would always be.

"Good night, hon." He scooted her legs inside and stepped back to swing the door closed. "Sleep well."

Later, as he lay in the back of the truck and listened to the soft hum of the semis while the drivers caught some shut-eye, he thought about the three feet that separated him from Ellie. It might as well have been three thousand feet. He wasn't about to do anything about the state she'd left him in. But in addition to the uncomfortable tightness of his jeans, he was confused. He'd thought he knew what he wanted when the season ended, but after spending this time with Ellie, he wasn't so sure anymore.

* * *

"Ellie, wake up."

Slowly she opened her eyes to bright sunlight. She'd fallen asleep about two hours outside of Austin, needing to rest after the sleepless night she'd spent.

"Feel better?" Chace asked, turning into the camping area near the fairgrounds.

She smiled and stretched her arms, getting the kinks out and wondering how he managed to sleep in the back of his truck so many times. Ready to suggest he ought to get a camper like hers, she spotted her own. "There's Ray," she said, pointing to their right.

Chace easily found a place near her rig and parked his own. Scrambling out, she hurried to Ray. "How bad was it?"

"Nothin' but a busted belt." He looked past her. "Chace, I need to talk to you 'bout somethin'."

Joining them, Chace slipped an arm around Ellie's waist. "You sure made good time. I thought we'd get here long before you."

Ray started to walk away and gestured for Chace to follow. "Like I told Miss Ellie, it was a busted belt. Didn't take no time at all and I drove straight on through."

Chace lingered, pulling her close for a moment, then followed. "That's a long drive. How's your hand?"

Ellie listened to Ray's answer, but she soon couldn't hear the two men's voices. Left to herself, she strolled to Chace's trailer to remove her horse. She'd sensed something different about Chace since they'd started out that morning, but before she could give it much thought, she heard her name being called and looked up. In a split second, she was running. "Matt! Brett!"

Brett grabbed her by the waist and swung her

around. "We were getting worried. We saw that guy with your rig. Who is he?"

She couldn't contain her joy at seeing her brothers. "He's a friend. I'll explain later. But what are you doing here? I didn't know you were coming."

Brett set her on her feet and looked at his older brother. "We wanted to surprise you."

Matt, who looked so much like their father that Ellie felt a stab of pain each time she saw him, came closer. "We've got some questions to ask you."

She looked from one to the other. "Questions? Is something wrong?"

Matt frowned and stuffed his hands in his pockets. "We got a call from your real estate friend," he answered, his voice full of disgust. "Told us he had an offer for the place and asked if we were interested in selling. I told him we had a sister who'd have to agree. He said you already had. What's going on, Ellie? Why are you doing this?"

Shocked that J.R. would go behind her back and contact her brothers, she wasn't sure what to say. "I'm trying to save your lives."

"When are you going to stop blaming yourself for something that wasn't your fault?" Brett asked her.

She ignored the question. They had never understood. They never would. "If you'll just listen—"

"The ranch may not be your home, big sister, but it's mine and Brett's." Matt stood glaring at her. He'd always been the stubborn one.

"And it'll kill you. Both of you," she replied, fixing her face in a hard mask. She loved her brothers, more than anything, but she wouldn't let her emotions get the better of her. She'd failed to save her parents. She couldn't fail with her brothers.

Shaking her head, she took a deep breath. "I wanted to save this conversation until the end of the season. J.R. never should have called you."

Matt's dark eyes narrowed. "But he did. And now we know. And we won't sell." He grabbed her arm and held it tight. "Do you hear? We won't sell our home."

Chapter Six

"Remember me sayin' I saw somethin' in the road when Miss Ellie broke down?" Ray asked as Chace followed him away from Ellie.

Chace nodded. "You figured it was her alternator belt."

Ray reached around and pulled a piece of black rubber out of his back pocket. "Sure was. I walked back to get it while the tow truck fella hooked up her rig. It was kinda tricky, what with the trailer and all."

Chace stared at the belt Ray handed him. "It's been cut."

"Yep. Looked to me like somebody cut it enough so she wouldn't get too far down the road before it tore the rest of the way."

Looking in the direction of Ellie's rig, Chace shook his head. "Who would want to do that?"

"Don't know," Ray answered. "But I thought you'd wanna know about it. You seem to be real taken with the little lady."

Chace suspected he knew exactly who might want to slow Ellie down. But he didn't know why. "Can you do some digging and find out if anybody saw somebody around her truck Sunday night or Monday morning?"

"Sure thing. I'll let you know soon as I find out anything."

Chace thanked him and started back to his truck. Should he warn Ellie? But who would he warn her about? J.R.? He didn't have any proof, and he sure didn't have any reason why the weasel would do such a thing. But he'd damn sure find out if it was J.R.

At his own truck, he tossed the belt in the back and went to find Ellie. Until he knew more, he wouldn't say anything. He'd just keep a closer eye on her.

Raised voices hurried him around his truck to the other side of her camper. She wasn't alone, and he didn't like the way the cowboy with her was holding on to her.

The look of shock on Ellie's face caused him to grab the man's shoulder and jerk him around. "You'd better think twice about what you're doing," he growled.

"You'd better mind your own business," the cowboy snarled in reply and didn't let go of her.

"I warned you." Chace pulled back his arm, intending to plant his fist in the cowboy's face, and was knocked back several steps when Ellie lunged at him.

"No, Chace! He's my brother."

Chace pulled his punch and stared at her, still holding a handful of the man's shirt in his other fist. "Huh?"

She pried his fingers from the shirt. "My brother, you fool." She glanced at the cowboy when Chace let go of him. "For heaven's sake, Matt. You've got people staring at us."

Matt ducked his head and looked at another man who resembled Ellie. Realization hit Chace that he'd come close to flattening Ellie's kin. Not the best way to get in her good graces.

She turned her back on him, and he reached out to stop her. "Look, I'm—"

"Forget it," she said with a dismissive wave and shook off his hand. "You always seem to show up at the worst times."

"When you need me most, you mean," Chace said with a grin. He extended his hand to Matt. "Chace Brannigan. Sorry I didn't ask questions first, but I'm always finding your sister in some kind of trouble."

Matt's eyes widened, and he took the offered hand. "Chace Brannigan, three-time National Saddle Bronc Champion?"

Chace nodded and turned to look at the fair-haired brother who stood staring at him. "If I'd seen you first, I'd have known you were related to Ellie."

The bigger version of her stuck out his hand. "Brett Warren. Matt got a little carried away. Usually he's pretty mellow."

Matt lowered his head and let out a long breath. "Sorry, Ellie, I didn't meant to grab you. But sometimes—"

"Like I said, forget it," she answered in a voice filled with love. "We'll talk about it later. Besides, you've got Chace Brannigan right here in front of you. I'd think you'd be full of questions. Both of you," she added with a smile.

"Just seein' him in the flesh is somethin'," Brett

replied. "We've followed your career for years, Mr. Brannigan."

"Call me Chace. And if you've followed very close, you know I've had my share of bad years."

"Not this year," Brett said, his eyes gleaming with admiration. "You're sittin' at the top of the heap. But then, to me and Matt you've always been the best."

"Matt and Brett tried rodeoing a few years back," Ellie explained. "It got to be too much, with the ranch and all."

Just by seeing them together, Chace could tell there was a lot of love among these people. From what Ellie had told him, her brothers weren't in favor of selling their ranch. But there was only one way to find out, and he didn't want her to know he was doing it.

"Is that Sky Dancer I hear kicking up a ruckus?" he asked, hoping to get a few minutes alone with Matt and Brett.

She sighed and gave her brothers a soft smile. "He's been cooped up in that trailer. I'd better get him out of there. Don't go away until I'm done."

"Would you mind checking on Redneck?" Chace asked, hopefully buying a little more time.

"Sure."

Chace felt the familiar hot wave wash over him as he watched her walk away, unable to tear his gaze from the view.

"What kind of trouble has she been into?" Matt asked when she was out of sight.

Turning back, Chace chose his words with care. "She's met a man whose intentions might not be all they seem."

"She never mentioned she was seeing anybody."

Hoping he was doing the right thing, Chace continued. "I think this has more to do with your ranch than it does with your sister's dating choices."

"She wants to sell the ranch," Matt said with disgust.

"So I've heard. Is that what you boys want?"

"Hell, no!" Matt said. "I'll admit, times haven't been the best lately. Cattle prices aren't what they ought to be."

"I understand that. I have a share in a ranch near here. I'm not involved much, but I know how tight things have been for ranchers."

"But we don't want to sell," Brett agreed.

Chace was glad to know he hadn't been wrong about them. "We've got to make this quick, before she gets back. But I know J.R. Staton, the real estate agent, and I'm pretty sure he's up to no good. Do you boys know if there might be oil on your land? I have a feeling that's what he might be after."

"It hasn't been surveyed or we'd know about it."

"Doesn't matter. They've got some new ways of checking on those things. Aerial photos, things like that. And if they've found any oil in the area, they can pretty well determine where there's more."

Matt rubbed his chin with one hand. "So you think that's what he's up to with our place?"

"Can't say for sure," Chace admitted. "But my advice is to check around to see if the land's been surveyed. You might ask Ellie if J.R.'s mentioned the buyer's name. I'd stake my life that he won't tell her because it's him. He doesn't have to divulge that, either. Not if he's set up a dummy corporation." He checked to make sure Ellie wasn't on her way back before he continued. "But do me a favor. Don't tell her you're doing anything. And don't let J.R. know you're checking into it.''

"String him along?" Brett asked.

"That'd be best until you know for sure where you stand.''

"We can do that," Matt assured him.

Reaching into his shirt pocket, Chace pulled out one of his cards. "Here's my cell phone number. Give me a call as soon as you find out anything. I'll try to talk some sense into her about selling the place.''

Matt was stuffing the card into his back pocket when Ellie returned. "The horses were doing fine, Chace. I can't imagine what you heard.''

He shrugged. "Must've been somebody else's horses.''

She turned to her brothers. "How long are you staying?"

"We have to head back as soon as we watch you ride," Matt answered. "Both of you," he added with a nod at Chace.

With a promise to meet her after her ride, the brothers said their goodbyes and left Ellie to Chace. "We need to talk," he told her, moving her closer.

"If it's about what happened last night, forget it." She tried to ease away from him, but he reached for her hand and kept her from leaving.

He shook his head and grinned at her. "Can't. And I'd wager you can't, either.''

"I've never been a betting woman. Life is enough of a risk. We'll talk later." She scrambled away from him before he could stop her.

He watched the rhythm of her hips, swaying back and forth, as she walked away. Damn! She did things to him that made him forget about every other woman he'd ever met. He'd give her a little time and catch up with her later.

Just the thought of holding her again and tasting her sweet kiss left him aching with wanting her. "Later, Ellie," he whispered to her retreating back.

Ellie waited, her heart pounding like the hooves of the horses in the arena, while the last two barrel racers took their places to try to beat her time. She was in the lead in the final round of the Austin County Rodeo. And she had to win. Second place wouldn't do it. To make it to National Finals, she had to be in the top fifteen money winners in the country. She was there, but just barely.

Her nerves drawn tight, she jumped when a pair of arms encircled her waist. She looked back to see Chace smiling encouragement.

"Hang in there," he said.

If only she could laugh and act as if she didn't care, as if it wasn't important to her. But lighthearted banter was foreign to her at that moment. The outcome was too important. Her future hinged on it.

All too aware of him, she knew she should pull away and step out of his embrace. But she couldn't do that, either. Even though she hated to admit it, she needed his strength and confidence, the warmth of his body and the steady beat of his heart in her ear.

Nodding, she swallowed her nervousness. "Thanks."

The next racer circled her horse behind the starting barrier, and Chace's arms tightened around Ellie when horse and rider took off, heading for the first barrel of the cloverleaf. Ellie held her breath. She didn't want the girl to do badly. She'd never wish that on anyone.

But this was important. One one-thousandth of a second could make a difference.

When the last barrel wobbled and fell, Ellie didn't know whether to laugh or cry. Hooves thundered in her direction, and she closed her eyes, thankful for the small break and sorry it had to happen to the other cowgirl. Emotions crowded in on her, but she pushed them aside. It wasn't over yet.

"You did your best, right?" Chace asked in a quiet voice.

"It was a good ride." And it was, in spite of the fact that Matt and Brett had had to leave as soon as it was over. They hadn't had a chance to talk about the sale of the ranch. She hadn't changed her mind. She still hoped she could change theirs.

"As long as you know you did your best, then don't worry about it." His warm words encouraged her.

She answered with a nod, but couldn't rid herself of the knot in her stomach as she focused her attention on the arena.

The last racer took her place, her prancing horse eager to do his job. The crowd quieted, knowing that this last ride would tell the story of the barrel racing winner for this rodeo.

Before Ellie could take a breath to steady herself, the racing team took off, making a quick, tight round of the barrel to the right, then heading for the left one. The figure eight completed with precision, the rider urged the horse for the third and farthest barrel. Execution was perfect, causing Ellie's heart to thud even harder. She watched the horse and rider speed toward her on the stretch.

Close. It would be so close.

When the time was announced and the winner

named, Ellie sagged against Chace, tears stinging her eyes.

"Go get your buckle," he told her, giving her a quick hug and sending her on her way into the arena.

In a daze, she received her prize, grinning, and then found herself outside the arena, standing in front of Chace again, unable to lasso the feelings bursting inside her.

"Feel better?" he asked, draping his arm around her shoulders.

She let loose with relieved laughter. "You can't imagine."

His laughter joined hers. "Yeah, I can."

She stared at the buckle in her hand while they walked away, Chace leading both her horse and his. "I just wish Matt and Brett could have stayed."

"They had work to do."

She twisted to frown at him. "That's my point. They seldom get away. They're always working."

"That's their choice. What's important to you isn't to them."

Pulling away, she stepped in front of him and brought him to a halt. "You just don't get it, Brannigan. *Life* is important."

He studied her, making her squirm under his intense stare. "Sure it is. And sometimes it's hard. Just like you're making it real hard for me to ask if you want to go celebrate."

She'd been so wrapped up in her own scores and outcome, she'd forgotten he had two wins of his own. "Sorry," she said, ducking her head. "I guess you do have reason to celebrate."

With one finger, he tipped up her chin, forcing her

to meet his gaze. "Then how 'bout going for a burger? Or whatever you want."

Her stomach somersaulted at the wanting in his eyes, but her own need frightened her. She couldn't let herself fall any more for this man. She hadn't been able to stop herself before, but she had to now. No matter how much he made her pulse quicken and her breath catch, she wasn't looking for a good time that would be over at the end of the season. That's all a man like Chace had to offer. The more time she spent with him, the harder it would be when they went their separate ways.

"It might be better if we didn't," she forced herself to say.

"We could go someplace fancy, similar to that place in Phoenix."

"No, that's not it. I just…" How could she lie and tell him she didn't want his company, when that's all she'd been yearning for since they'd met? Just knowing he'd be at this rodeo had pushed her to drive faster and longer than usual. But he was so wrong for her.

As she turned to walk away, he put his arm around her again. Stopping, she lifted his hand from her shoulder and dropped it.

"What did I do?" he asked, coming after her when she strode on toward her trailer.

"You're looking for something I can't give you."

"What? A burger and a beer? Maybe fries on the side?"

"You know what I mean," she said, avoiding a glance in his direction when he caught up with her.

They reached her stock trailer, and she took the reins from him. With practiced ease, she unsaddled

Sky Dancer and, after giving him a quick brush down, led him inside.

"I get it," Chace said when she'd closed the door to the trailer. "Okay, no hands. I promise to be a gentleman. Now, can we go celebrate?"

She didn't doubt he'd behave. He wasn't the kind of man who wouldn't. But being with him was more than she could deal with. She hadn't forgotten the kisses they'd shared.

"You could tell me why you want to sell the ranch," he said, his voice soft and seductive in her ear.

A spiral of heat curled in her, but she kept her back to him. "Why should I?"

Leaning closer, his breath whispered across her cheek. "Maybe I could tell you why your brothers are against it."

She spun around to face him, folding her arms on her chest and glaring at him. "I knew it. You're on their side."

"There's always two sides to a story. And you weren't going to tell me theirs. Now it's your turn."

Even though the thought of asking for help left her cold, she considered it. If she could convince Chace that selling was the right thing to do, she'd have him on her side. Maybe he'd be willing to talk to her brothers and tell them she was right. They admired him. They might listen to him.

"Okay. Let's celebrate."

Chace watched as Ellie dipped another fry in a blob of ketchup. He had discovered at Reba's that he enjoyed watching Ellie eat. Unlike other women, she didn't pick at her food. How she stayed so small had him puzzled. He could circle her waist with his hands with little effort. Sitting across from her in the booth of a local burger place, he wished he could do just that. And more. But it would have to wait.

Shoving her nearly empty plate aside, Ellie leaned her elbows on the table and propped her chin in her hands. "There's something I wanted to explain to you. I know you think I'm wrong about selling the ranch, but what you don't understand is that I'm not doing it for selfish reasons."

"I didn't say you were." He watched the wrinkles of worry between her eyes deepen and wished he could smooth them away with his fingers. When he'd finished doing that, he would take her in his arms and kiss her until she'd forgotten all about her brothers and the ranch.

"They'll work themselves into an early grave," she continued. "I saw my parents do it. They never went anywhere, never did anything, just stayed on that ranch until it took their lives. And I couldn't save them. I tried, but I couldn't. I can't let that happen to my brothers. If it takes selling the ranch, I will."

From the shimmer in her eyes, he knew a few glib words about a ranch being a man's life work wouldn't change her mind. And he wasn't ready to risk telling her that it would be his work soon. Not until he could sort through his feelings for her.

He reached across the table and took her hand, hoping to at least comfort her. "What happened?"

Tears filled her eyes. "The stock were always so important. When some of the cattle were missing, they went to check the creek that had frozen over. I know those animals were our livelihood, but—" She shook her head as if in denial and blinked away the tears.

He could see she'd bottled things up for too long. This was something she needed to get out. He squeezed her hand to encourage her and waited for her to continue.

"I'd just turned eighteen. The boys were in town at a basketball game. When my folks didn't come home after an hour, I saddled my horse and went looking for them. The ice had broken." She stopped to take a shaky breath. "I was too late."

He closed his eyes against the pain he felt for her. She'd only been a kid, and she obviously still carried deep scars from the loss. He knew what it was to lose a parent. He'd lost both of his, too, although he hadn't told her that, yet. If he could have spared her the pain, he would have. All he could do was try to ease it and offer comfort—and without taking her in his arms as he wanted.

"It's because of the memories," he said, opening his eyes. "That's why you don't care about the ranch."

"I don't want to see the same thing happen to my brothers that happened to our folks," she answered with a stubborn but wobbly tilt to her chin. "Even if there aren't any accidents, the ranch will kill them. They just can't see it."

The grip she had on his hand was proof enough of how badly she wanted them away from the place. Smoothing his thumb across hers, he smiled. "They're grown men with lives of their own."

Her eyes burned with a deep need as she rushed on. "I need to get them away from there before something happens to them. Before there's even more unhappiness."

"Ranching doesn't cause unhappiness, hon," he

tried. "It's hard work, I'll admit. But it makes some people happy. I think it does your brothers."

She shook her head and pressed her lips in a stubborn line.

"Why don't you let them buy you out?"

Her eyes flashed anger, and she pulled her hand away. "For one thing, they don't have the money to do it. And even if they did, I don't want them there. Can't you understand that?"

Chace nodded. He could see she'd never gotten over the death of her parents, but she was being unreasonable by blaming it on the ranch. "You have to understand that your brothers' lives are their own. It's their decision."

She stood, wadding up a paper napkin and tossing it on the table. "That's your opinion."

When she turned and walked away, Chace dug in his pocket and tossed enough money on the table to cover the bill and a tip before going after her. He caught up with her as she stepped outside, and took her arm. "I wasn't trying to make you mad."

She pulled away and kept going. "You were just telling me what to do. In a nice way, of course."

Damn stubborn woman! He took hold of her again, but didn't let go, steering her toward his truck. "You are, undoubtedly, the most pigheaded woman I've ever met."

She lifted her chin. "How noble of you to say so."

"Ellie, be reasonable—"

She came to a sudden halt and spun on him. "Why? All of my life men have told me what to do. They always thought they knew what was best for me. If it hadn't been for the fact that I was legally an adult,

Matt and Brett never would have let me travel the country alone. But I did, and I've done just fine.

"I know what's best for them, Chace. And I know I can convince them of it. When we sell the ranch, they'll have enough money to be comfortable and do what they want to do."

He couldn't back down on his promise to her brothers to try to make her see reason. "What if they want to ranch?"

"There are other things they can do. Things they like."

"You won't give up, will you?"

"I *can't*." She grabbed his arm, her fingers digging into the muscle. "They're all I have, Chace."

He saw the fear in her eyes, but he didn't know how to help her. "You can't force them to sell the ranch, Ellie."

Her eyes blazed with determination and passion. "I won't have to. I'll make them see the wisdom in it. And you can help me do that. Help me make them see—"

"No." He took a step back, shaking his head.

She froze, her eyes wide with disbelief. As she let go of him, her shoulders drooped in defeat. "I should've known."

He wanted to help her, but what she was asking went against his principles. Her brothers would never agree, and that left her no option as far as he could see. "Where do Finals figure into this?"

"Whatever I win, however small, I can quit competing and settle down."

"What if it isn't enough?"

Her gaze hooked his. "I'll find a way."

A sliver of fear snaked up his spine. "And where does J.R. Staton fit into this?"

Her eyes narrowed. "I don't have to answer that."

She left him standing and walked to his truck where she waited for him. "Can we go now?" she asked when he caught up with her.

He nodded, the taste of fear in his mouth. But he didn't know how to stop it.

Ellie remained quiet during their drive back to the fairgrounds. She couldn't believe Chace had refused to help her. The one person she'd dared to count on. Never again. Lowering her guard to allow J.R. to assist her in selling the ranch was one thing, but Chace was different. She'd made the choice to ask for his help. She wouldn't repeat the mistake.

Although he might make her feel things she suspected she never would with anyone else, she'd forget him. A cowboy who roamed the country riding broncs was out of the question. No matter how fast he made her heart beat or how hot he made her blood race through her veins, she didn't love him. Not yet, anyway.

She knew a little about love. The love she had for her brothers. The love she'd had for her parents. When she'd told Chace about the accident, the memories had flooded back, along with her dad's last words to her, and how she'd failed to save him. She fought the images from her mind, once again hiding the guilt she still battled.

To win the fight, she turned her mind to the one thing that seemed to bother Chace. "What do you have against J.R.?" she asked, breaking the silence as they sped through the night.

He turned to look at her, a scowl on his face. "What do you have against *me?*"

Afraid to look at him for fear he might read something in her expression, she stared out the window. "That's beside the point."

"Nope. You just don't want to admit that there's something going on between us."

She turned to him, determined to put a stop to a topic she didn't want to discuss. "Why would you think that? I've done everything to let you know that I'm not interested in that sort of thing."

"And how did you do that, Ellie?"

The grin he shot her made her heart turn cartwheels. Hot waves of desire swept through her at the sound of his husky voice, and she sat up straighter. "Why can't you forget about that?"

"Because I don't want to."

They reached the fairground parking, and he turned in, making his way slowly to the rodeoers area. Three trucks down from hers, he pulled into an empty space and killed the engine.

He turned to look at her. "Now answer my question."

Pivoting away from him in the seat, she avoided his demand. "I don't remember what it was."

She listened to the sound of his door opening, heard him slide from the seat and jumped at the sound of the door closing. Before she realized what he was doing, he'd circled the truck and yanked open her door.

Placing his hands at her waist, he lifted her from the truck and set her on her feet. He slid his hands around her and pulled her against him, his mouth mere inches from hers. "Is this the sort of thing you were referring to?"

She didn't have a chance to answer before he took possession of her lips. Intending to push him away, she put her hands against his chest. But instead of the shove she planned to give him, her body betrayed her. Clinging to him, she pressed against him, needing the feel of him. She opened her lips to his drugging kiss, meeting his tongue with hers, and forgot everything else around them.

After endless minutes he tore his mouth from hers, and his ragged breath whispered at her ear. "Tell me what you have against me. Is it because I make you as crazy as you make me?"

Unable to answer, she buried her face in his chest. Confusion brought tears to her eyes. She couldn't be feeling these things. He was cowboy through and through. The lure of rough stock and the grit of dust ran through his veins as sure as the blood that coursed through them.

Her parents had loved the ranch with the same passion. In return, it had given them years of hardship, little money at times and more hard work than anyone should ever have to do. For what? To lose their lives one cold, winter night for a few head of cattle. Chace was the same with rodeo. She refused to spend the rest of her life as a gypsy, following him from rodeo to rodeo. He could never give it up.

"I have to go, Chace," she said, forcing herself to move out of his arms.

"No." He reached for her, but she twisted away. His sigh was one of frustration. "We need to talk about this. The season is almost over."

She felt the autumn chill in the Texas night and wrapped her arms around her middle. By the hard line of his jaw and the determination in his eyes, she knew she had to see this through. "All right," she said. "But can we go back to my camper?"

He took her arm. "Let's go."

A chill crept into her heart. She needed time to find a way to tell him the truth without letting him know how much it hurt her to say it, but he wasn't going to give her that time.

Chace's heart thudded in his chest. If this was about J.R., he'd have to tell her about her cut alternator belt. But he didn't want to, until he knew for sure. What he wanted was to know what was scaring her away from him. He knew she felt something for him. A woman who didn't want any part of a man didn't melt in his arms the way she did in his. Nor did her eyes darken to almost black with desire. The air sizzled when the two of them were anywhere near each other.

He could understand why she wanted to sell the ranch. What she'd been through with her parents' accident would leave scars on anybody. Hell, he had his own. But why was she going to stop barrel racing? She'd proven she was one of the best. Maybe not National Championship material yet, but in a year or two she could be. She had what it took. Why would she quit now, when she was so close?

As they reached her camper, his tension mounted. Beside him Ellie walked with her usual determination. The silence gnawed at him.

"Where are you headed in the morning?" he asked, hoping she'd be somewhere near so they could spend some time together.

"Little Rock."

His heart hit his knees. He was going in the opposite direction. "We're headed to Billings. Ray and me."

A floodlight lit her camper with enough light for him to see her. Dark circles he hadn't noticed earlier shadowed her cheeks beneath eyes that shimmered with what looked like unshed tears.

Unable to keep away from her any longer, he reached out and touched his finger to her cheek. "You okay?"

"Sure, I'm fine." But her voice trembled, betraying her words, and she didn't look at him.

It bothered the hell out of him that he wouldn't see her for close to two weeks. Somebody needed to keep an eye on her. He wouldn't be able to.

"After Little Rock?" he asked, hoping she'd say North Dakota. He'd promised an old buddy he'd be there for a wedding at the rodeo grounds. Steve had asked him to stand up as best man, and Chace had assured him nothing would keep him from it.

Ellie didn't move to look at him. "Casper."

He braced himself against the camper at the news. If one of them didn't make Finals, he might not see her again. He had to find a way to keep her from selling her ranch and making some other damn fool mistake.

And he needed to know what it was about this woman that made him feel this way. She wasn't his responsibility. She didn't want his help. But he couldn't stop himself from wanting to help her. From wanting to see her safe and happy. From wanting *her*. If it was because of the challenge she presented, he'd know soon. If it wasn't...

He tried not to show that it mattered that they'd be almost three hundred miles apart. "Casper's a good one."

Her teeth sank into her bottom lip and she nodded.

"It'll pay a lot, if I can win. It'd give me a solid spot for Finals."

Moving closer, he slipped an arm around her waist and pulled her toward him. "You'll do great."

She met his gaze, the warmth in her eyes gone. "We're not here to wish each other good luck. We're here to get some things out in the open."

Cold dread seeped into his body, and he realized that the answer to his question could wait. He'd see her in Las Vegas, and they could talk it out there. *If* they both made it to Finals. But this wasn't the time to press the issue. Not the way she was acting.

"Look, Ellie, you don't have to—"

She jerked her head up, her eyes glittering with cold determination. "No, Chace. You've come to my rescue too many times. I owe you an answer to your question."

"You don't owe me anything. I wanted to help. I still do."

"Do you?"

She was slipping away from him. The thought left a tightening band around his chest. This might be his last chance. "I'll help any way I can, hon. Just name it."

She nodded and took a deep breath before locking her gaze with his. "Then let me go, Chace. You don't fit in the life I have planned. Not anywhere. And I don't fit into yours."

He stared at her, pain gnawing at him. "Maybe you should let me in on this plan of yours."

"It's simple," she said with a shrug and looked away. "I sell the ranch for the best price I can get and make sure Matt and Brett are set up someplace where I know they'll be safe."

He didn't doubt for a minute she didn't believe she could do it. And if he hadn't met her brothers, he might believe it, too. But it was clear to him that, whether she could convince them or not, she'd never return to the ranch.

"And you'll move to the city," he said, the words bitter.

"Yes. Tulsa, maybe. Dallas. Maybe north. I don't know for sure."

None of that answered the question that had kept him awake all night. "Why?"

The truth he didn't want to face shone in her eyes.

"No cowboys, Chace. I made a vow the night I found my daddy and mama in that creek that as soon as I could, I'd leave, permanently, and never go back. I want a house in the city—any city—where I won't have to worry about drought or floods or cattle or feed prices."

"But why quit rodeo?"

"Barrel racing was all I knew, and it got me off the ranch. Not just that ranch, but any ranch. I don't want that kind of life. I won't wake up someday and find myself old and worn-out with nothing to show for it. Or not live long enough."

"It wouldn't have to be that way," he reasoned. But her words had cut deep. The Brannigans were ranchers. He'd given his word that he'd retire to help with the Triple B. Trey was counting on him. And Chace needed to do it. Ellie might have her demons and dreams, but he had his own.

"What about J.R.?" he asked.

She stared at him, her eyes wide. "I don't have any plans concerning J.R., except for him to get me the best price for the ranch."

"But he might have plans."

Ellie shook her head. "You're wrong, Chace."

"Am I?" He stuffed his hands in his pockets to keep from grabbing her and shaking some sense into her. But, in the long run, it wouldn't do any good. He was a cowboy. And that was the one thing, whether he rodeoed or not, that he would always be. Years ago he'd left, not content with being confined on the Triple B. But he'd made his choice and now he was making another one. It would be better if he cut his losses with Ellie now, before he was in too deep. He never should have let it go this far.

Bitterness rose in his throat, and he choked it back. Pushing away from the camper, he stood in front of her, looking down. "I wish you the very best, Ellie Warren. Maybe you'll change your mind someday."

"Chace," she called to him when he'd turned to walk away.

He stopped, not wanting to look at her, but he glanced back, anyway.

"If it means anything to you, I wish it were different."

He kept going.

Chapter Seven

"I can't believe I wanted to be here," Ellie muttered to herself. Readying Sky Dancer for their final ride of the season finale in Casper, Wyoming, she tried to shake off the worst case of nerves she could ever remember having. Only the competition at National Finals could be more intense than it was in Casper. Her win in Little Rock had made this a do or die situation. She'd never really dreamed she would make it this far. "If I make it through this without an ulcer, it'll be a miracle."

She'd ridden against most of her competition at one time or another throughout the season. There would still be a few from back East where she hadn't been since early spring, or from Canada, where some of the best riders competed. But she knew what she was up against.

And she was two one-thousandths of a second behind the leader going into the final round.

Her hands trembled as she checked the cinch for the

third time. "We have to do it this time, fella," she whispered to her horse. "There won't be any more chances."

"That horse won't let you down."

She turned to see Reba walking toward her and attempted a smile. "I hope I don't let *him* down. Right now, I have more faith in him than I have in myself."

Reba reached her and put an arm around her shoulders. "You'll do your best, just like you always do."

"I hope my best is good enough. My other times weren't—"

"Those were other rides, girl," Reba reminded her. "Tonight it's this one. You ride Sky Dancer like you've been doin' all year and you won't have anythin' to worry about."

Ellie had to smile at her friend's faith. "You're right. It's just another race, that's all." And if she kept telling herself that long enough, pretty soon she'd believe it. This would be the most important ride of her life. It was now or never.

Reba walked with her to the gate. "I'm gonna find myself a seat somewhere. I'll be the one yellin' the loudest."

"Thanks, Reba. You're the best."

After a hug from her friend, Ellie mounted and took her place with the other contestants waiting their turn. She heard her name announced and rotated her shoulders to relax the muscles that had been tightening all day. Taking several deep breaths, she forced her heart to slow enough to allow her to think clearly. It would take all her concentration to make this a good ride.

"Ellie Warren is our last barrel racer. Give this little cowgirl a warm welcome," the announcer said over the PA system.

She nudged her horse into the arena and stopped, facing away from the barrels. She heard, but didn't think about, what the announcer was saying.

"Ellie hails from near Tulsa, Oklahoma. She's in second place behind Amy Strong. This ride will tell if Ellie will be going to the National Finals Rodeo in Las Vegas in December."

A calm came over her, and her breathing evened out. With a flick of the reins, she turned Sky Dancer, and they headed for the first barrel. She felt the perfect execution he made of it, then urged him toward the next barrel before making the run for the third one. Sky Dancer moved with grace and speed, cutting the turns close, but not too close. Once they'd rounded the last barrel, she gave a quick kick of her heels, and they sprinted back for the finish line.

In the background she could hear the crowd cheering. As she pulled up after breaking the timer, she held her breath, waiting for her time. It had been a good ride, but she wouldn't know for sure how good until she heard.

"Well, folks," the announcer drawled. "Looks like we have a new champ here tonight. Ellie Warren just beat Amy Strong's time by one one-thousandth of a second. Let's give her a round of applause and wish her the best in Vegas."

Ellie went limp and nearly dropped the reins. The arena spun around her as she waved to the spectators before leaving the arena. She'd done it. She'd really done it!

Once outside the gate, she was swarmed with well-wishers congratulating her on her win. A good sport, Amy was the most vocal and nicest of all of them. Ellie quickly reminded herself that things could have been different. One barrel taken too tight, and she would have added five seconds to her time, putting her way down in the pack.

But she hadn't. She'd given it her best, just like Reba had said she would. And she felt wonderful!

Breaking loose from the crowd, she slid from her horse and whispered a private thank-you to him. It took not only a good rider but a good horse to do well. She led him in the direction of the trailer, praising him and not caring if anyone heard her.

She'd have been on top of the world if it hadn't been for the memory of her last conversation with Chace still haunting her. She missed him, more than she cared to admit, and she regretted that she'd had to say what she'd said. But his last words kept coming back to her. She wouldn't change her mind—couldn't change it. She could never live on the ranch. The memories, even when she infrequently visited, were too much for her to bear.

"Hey, Ellie."

For a moment her heart stood still, then she thought she'd imagined the one voice she'd secretly been wishing to hear. Whirling around, she saw Chace moving in her direction through the maze of people. She hadn't expected to see him again, except for maybe an accidental meeting in Vegas if she made Finals. She sure hadn't dreamed of seeing him here with a grin on his face like the one he wore now. Without a doubt, it was for her.

She dropped the reins to ground tie Sky Dancer and keep him in place, then gave him a quick pat. Within seconds she launched herself into Chace's arms.

Laughing, he scooped her up and spun her around. "I told you I'd put my money on you."

"When did you get here?" she asked when he stopped, her head spinning from more than just the swinging.

"Just in time to see you ride. We finished in Bismarck yesterday and headed out this morning."

Still in his arms, she gazed up at him and let the joy of seeing him fill her. After what she'd said in Austin, she hadn't expected him to care. Now she couldn't stop her happiness that he hadn't taken her seriously. "How'd you and Ray do? Did you win? What about bronc riding?"

"Second in roping and first in broncs," he said with a wink. "I guess you'll have to put up with me in Vegas."

Vegas. The word sent a thrill through her. "I'm having a hard time believing I'm really going. I've dreamed about it for so long."

"You deserve it," he said, his voice deep and husky. "And this."

Ellie saw it coming and knew she should stop it, but when he bent to kiss her, the only thing she wanted was to feel his lips on hers. His arms tightened around her and she slid her hands to his shoulders, where she could feel his strength. The kiss made her knees weak, but he held her close as he plundered her mouth.

And then it was over. He held her for a moment longer before setting her on her feet. Taking a step away, he tipped his hat back and looked at her. "You ready to celebrate?"

If the celebration includes more of that, she wanted to say. She wanted to tell him she'd like nothing better than to celebrate with him until dawn, but she'd promised to meet Reba and Nate later. "I've already made plans and need to stick around."

He raised one dark eyebrow before he pulled his hat lower to hide his eyes. "I should've figured."

She smiled at his disappointment. It was obvious that, no matter what they'd said to each other in Austin, he still cared. If only she didn't care so much. "I'm sure Reba and Nate would be happy if you joined us."

When he looked at her, his grin reached from ear to ear. Relief shone in his eyes before they dimmed. "Anybody else?"

She shook her head.

Grabbing her hand, he tugged her toward the arena. "If I'm invited to this shindig, I guess I'd better hang around. Let's find a couple of seats and watch the bull riders."

"I have to put Sky Dancer up first," she reminded him, a little disappointed that they wouldn't spend the time alone.

"We can make quick work of that with two of us."

Glad for the company, she led him in the direction of her trailer. He listened patiently while she chattered about the nerves and doubts she'd had about doing well, giving her the opportunity to rid herself of her pent-up energy. By the time they finished the grooming, she'd almost come down to earth and felt more like herself. Just having Chace around made everything right.

"Sounds like they're still riding bulls," he said, while she secured the trailer.

"There were a lot of entries."

Once she'd bidden Sky Dancer good-night, she turned to Chace. She couldn't deny the pleasure this short time with him gave her. He understood how she felt. He'd admitted that he, too, often went into a ride with self-doubts and even a small amount of fear. He made her feel normal when she'd been feeling completely unnormal, wanted when she'd been feeling isolated, cared about when she'd felt alone. With Chace she felt at peace. Oh, her hormones might rage at his very touch, sending lightning bolts flashing through her, and her heart might beat quicker at the sound of his voice, but along with that, she knew she didn't have to say or do anything to impress him. She didn't want to let the night end. And she didn't want to share this time with anyone but him.

With no resistance from her, he pulled her into his arms. "Do you really want to watch the bull riders?" he asked, as if he'd read her mind.

"I have some sandwiches and a couple of beers in the camper," she said. "A little ice cream, too."

"Ice cream and beer?" he asked with a grin that melted her to her toes. "Is that an invitation?"

She managed an awkward shrug. "Okay, it's not gourmet. But we could wait for Reba and Nate there. If Reba doesn't find me when the rodeo's over, she'll come to the camper."

"Couldn't ask for a better menu." He stole another kiss, this one gentle and brief but promising much more. "Or company."

She melted at his words and had to move to keep from asking him to kiss her again. "Come on, then," she said, taking his hand and tugging him along. "But I'm warning you, you'll have to fight me for the ice cream."

As they made their way to her camper, he laced his fingers with hers. "What kind is it? I'm particular."

"Rocky road."

"Good thing for you I'm a cherry-macadamia-nut man."

Nerves that had been stretched tight for too long snapped, sending her into a fit of giggles that didn't stop, even when they reached her camper. At her door, laughter made it difficult to dig the key out of her pocket. Chace sighed and pushed her hand aside to slip his fingers into her pocket. She let out a gasp at the intimate gesture and drew his gaze, while he pulled the key out with two fingers.

They stood, looking at each other, neither moving, and then he spoke, his voice rough in the darkness. "Maybe we should have that ice cream first."

She felt herself sway toward him and had to force herself to take a step back. There would be time enough later to see where this might lead. Turning quickly, she fumbled the key in the lock with trembling fingers and pulled the door open. She was all too aware of him behind her as they stepped up into the camper. She should have known better than to bring him here. The small, enclosed space intensified the electricity he set off in her.

"Have a seat," she said with only a slight tremor in her voice. She could feel his eyes on her as she opened the refrigerator to pull out the plastic-wrapped sandwiches she'd made to keep herself busy that afternoon. She hadn't dreamed she'd be sharing them with Chace. In fact, she hadn't expected to see him again at all. But he'd dropped back into her life when she needed someone the most. Because of their rodeo experiences, he understood her better than anyone ever had. If only he could understand her need to get away from the ranch.

"How'd you know ham and cheese is my favorite?'' he asked when she joined him at the table with two cans of beer.

''I didn't. It's all I had.''

''Must be fate.''

She looked up to see bright-blue eyes darken to navy, causing her heart to thud unmercifully.

He was the first to glance away. ''So Finals is your last rodeo?''

She bit her lip and stared down at the table in front of her, unseeing. She hoped they wouldn't get into a battle again. She'd believed he'd been sincere about wanting to help. But help from a man meant letting him take matters into his own hands, then having him reason it away by saying he was only helping. She'd been a fool to ask for his. He'd refused her. She didn't want to explain any more to him.

''It's time to set down some roots,'' she said, more to herself than to him. ''Time to retire.''

''Same here.''

Jerking her head up, she stared at him. To her surprise he was calmly eating his sandwich. A statement like that was far from matter-of-fact, but that's the way he appeared. ''What do you mean?''

He finished the beer she'd given him and smiled at her. ''I'm retiring after Finals, too.''

Stunned by his news, she slid her untouched beer across the table to him. ''I don't believe you.''

He pushed the can back. ''Keep it. You look like you need it.''

She shook her head and returned it. ''You can't retire, Chace. You're in your prime.''

''I'm thirty-three years old, hon.'' He reached for her hand and held it, sending a river of excitement through her. ''I've had more injuries and broken bones than you'd want to hear about. It's hard enough to get out of bed in the morning, let alone climb on a horse week after week.''

"That could be because you sleep in the back of the truck," she reminded him, trying her best to ignore her body's response to his touch.

Shaking his head, he chuckled. "Maybe that's part of it. But there are other things besides riding broncs and roping calves for a few bucks.''

"Like what? What will you do?''

Smoldering heat replaced the laughter in his eyes. "What do you think I'd be good at?''

She shook her head, ignoring the flames skipping through her body. She couldn't see him as anything other than what he was—a rodeo cowboy. A man who chased gold buckles and winners' purses.

He released her hand and leaned back in the seat, studying her. "My brother, Trey, is dead-set on turning the family cattle ranch into a dude ranch. And I'm one hundred percent against it.''

She could barely breathe. "*Family* ranch?''

He nodded, and the smile he gave her didn't reach his eyes.

More stunned than ever, she searched to understand what he was getting at. "What's wrong with a dude ranch?''

His broad shoulders moved in a shrug. "Probably nothing, but the idea of strangers traipsing all over the Triple B just doesn't sit right with me.''

"How big is it?''

"About a hundred thousand acres.''

She stared at him, unable to speak for a moment. The ranch had to be among the biggest spreads in Texas. "You *own* all that?''

"The three of us." His brows dipped in a frown. "Us and the bank, that is. At least until Finals are over."

Things began to come together, and she wasn't liking it. With sudden insight she realized she'd been hoping deep in her heart that things might change. That Chace would care for her—love her—and someday leave rodeo behind. If that happened, there'd be a chance for some kind of future together.

She couldn't believe she'd let herself dream. Rodeo was bad enough, but— "You're going to retire so you can ranch."

"That's about it."

Propping her elbows on the table, she pressed her face into her hands. "No wonder you're so set against me selling the ranch. You're a rancher."

"Not a real one. Not yet. Trey's been doing all the work for years. The money I've earned is what's kept it going the past couple of years. Just like you."

Ellie felt as though the earth had opened up and she'd fallen into the crack. The hope that she hadn't dared to think about shattered around her, causing an ache deep in her soul. Dreams didn't come true by magic. Hadn't she learned that?

"Our situations are different," she said, pushing herself to her feet and standing on shaking legs.

"Are they?"

She nodded and turned around so he couldn't see her holding back the tears that threatened to give away her true feelings. "I lost my folks on the ranch. It brings nothing but bad memories for me. And I don't want the same thing to happen to my brothers."

"Sounds simple enough. But it isn't, and you know it. We both know it. I lost my folks on the Triple B."

She turned to look at him, aching for him, but she couldn't give in. "It's different."

"Nope. My mom died when I was seven. Aneurysm. We were too far out to get help in time. And years later my dad, in the best physical shape he'd ever been in, fell from a horse. Heart attack." Chace's Adam's apple bobbed when he swallowed, and he took a deep breath. "I wasn't there when it happened. I'd taken off for the rodeo, instead of staying like a good son would have. Guilt can do some heavy damage, same as shock."

She knew the kind of damage he was talking about. She knew, firsthand, about guilt. "Oh, Chace, I'm sorry."

Before she could move to offer comfort, he stood and pulled her into his arms. "I just want you to be careful of what you're doing. Once the ranch is gone, it's gone. For all of you. I know what it's like to almost lose it."

She didn't feel the same way he obviously did. She never would. But she wouldn't tell him so. "What happened?"

"My great-great-grandfather and another man were partners. It didn't take long before greed caused a rift, and the feud began. A generation later, oil was found on a part of the land the other family had been claiming was theirs. It wasn't theirs, but they were never convinced. The feud has lasted for four generations and came to an end not long ago. And the man who lost is still after it." He hesitated before continuing. "You'll never meet a more mean-spirited person than him. Greedy, just like his family."

Anger burned in his eyes, and she pressed her hand to his cheek. "It must have been hard."

"We managed. We won a few fights and lost a few, but through it all, we kept the Triple B and gained their share, too. I got tired of the battle and left. After Dad died, the wells that had kept the ranch going through some hard times went dry. Jim—" He shook his head and his mouth twisted in a sad smile. "He's never forgiven us for having what he sees as his, and he still believes there's oil, but there isn't. The oil doesn't matter to Dev and Trey and me. The ranch does."

Laying her cheek against his chest, Ellie sighed. "It means a lot to you."

"That's why Finals are so important to me. I'll take my winnings and sink them into the ranch. We'll make it the best in Texas."

She understood, but her spirits sank even farther. He might be leaving rodeo, but when he did, he'd be a rancher. To her, living on a ranch meant an early death. And she'd fallen in love with this man....

There was a knock on the door before it swung open. "Ellie, are you— Oh, I sure didn't mean to interrupt."

Gathering her wits, Ellie stepped away from Chace and pasted a smile on her face. "You didn't, Reba. We have ice cream. There's plenty for you and Nate."

"Nope, not tonight," Reba said with a glance at Chace. "Nate's plumb tuckered out. I was gonna ask if we couldn't do our celebratin' tomorrow before we hit the road. Maybe a big breakfast somewhere."

"Good idea, Reba," Chace said. "Ellie's pretty worn-out, too."

Ellie looked at him but said nothing. It was time for the evening to come to an end. Being with him only made her long for things that couldn't be. She needed to be alone.

"You come with us in the morning, Chace," Reba invited him with a wink. "The more the merrier, you know."

"Ray and I plan to be gone by sunup."

"Oh," Reba said, her disappointment clear. "We'd sure like to have you. But we'll see Ellie in the morning."

Ellie forced a cheerfulness she didn't feel. "You sure will. Bye, Reba. Hope Nate gets rested up."

"He'll have a month to do that before we come watch you both at Finals." With a wave and a grin she was gone.

In the silence that followed, Chace pulled Ellie back into his arms. "Where are you spending your time during the break?"

"The ranch."

Tipping her chin up with one knuckle, he caught her gaze. "Come to the Triple B with me, Ellie. It's in the Banderas. The country is beautiful. You can rest or practice or whatever you want. I'll even throw in a truckload of rocky road," he added with a smile.

Her heart wrenched at the thought of never seeing him again. Finals would be the end of it. The realization caused an ache she would always carry with her, but she had to be realistic and think of her future. "I'm sorry, Chace. I can't. I have to get back and convince Matt and Brett to sell."

His hand dropped, and his arm stiffened around her. "You're still bent on that? Can't you see—"

"I see that we're on different sides. We're after different things." Her throat tightened with tears she couldn't shed, and she couldn't say any more.

"And what if Matt and Brett won't agree?"

"I'll find another way."

"You could still race," he suggested. "Matt told me you sent most of your winnings back to the ranch. You could still do that."

Ellie attempted a laugh. "What little winnings there've been. No, Chace, this is it. I've spent the past year giving it my all. This is the best I can do."

"You're going to National Finals. That's nothing to laugh at."

"I'm thrilled about that. Please, believe me. But we both know I won't finish in the top of the money winners."

"Maybe not this year, but—"

"No— No more years."

"Then come to the ranch," he repeated. "Forget about Matt and Brett and selling. We'll work something out."

Her eyes searched his for the truth. Did he love her? She couldn't be sure. He was only offering her a little time with him. But that time would have to end. And then it would be even harder to walk away.

It was time he knew the truth. He needed to understand the reason she had to sell the ranch—had to see the dangers she saw, even though he might walk away sooner because of it.

"I can't face life on a ranch. It was my fault my parents died in that creek. I couldn't save them."

His arms tightened around her. "Accidents are nobody's fault, hon."

Tears stung her eyes, and she shook her head. "But if I'd gone out sooner—"

"You can't know if it would've made a difference."

Burying her face in his broad chest, she took a deep but shaky breath and let the memories pour into her. "I couldn't pull them out. My dad— For a few moments, my dad was still with me. Just long enough to tell me—to tell me—"

"What?" Chace whispered, his lips moving in her hair.

She knew she had to say it. Maybe if she did, she could free herself from the memory. But the pain made her falter.

"What did he say, hon?" he urged in a voice so gentle it made her want to weep.

The words that had haunted her for years, finally came out. "He said, 'Not your fault, little bit.'"

He held her even closer, the strength of his arms cradling her, but it gave her no comfort. Saying the words out loud hadn't helped. Nothing ever would.

He stroked her hair, and when he spoke his voice was low and soothing. "So that's it. Now I understand why you didn't want me calling you that. It wasn't your fault, hon. You have to believe that."

"If only I'd gone looking earlier—"

"No. You can't blame yourself." He held her away and forced her to look at him. "You didn't know. There's nothing wrong in that. You did what you could."

"Did I?" she asked, voicing the doubt that had tortured her since that night.

"Yes. Believe me."

But Chace hadn't been there. He hadn't heard her father's words, hadn't seen him take his last breath. "I can't let anything happen to my brothers. I can't go back to life on a ranch, where it could happen again."

"Everything has dangers."

She shook her head. "Not like ranching. I have to get my brothers away from it. And I have to get away. I have plans, remember?"

Dropping his arms from around her, he jammed his hands in his pockets. "Right. How could I forget? I don't fit your pretty picture of life in the city. But you know what they say. Be careful what you wish for. You just might get it."

Before she could answer, he'd gone. Sinking onto the seat where he'd sat at the table, she covered her face with her hands.

He would never understand. She'd lost her parents to the dangers of the ranch, and she hadn't been able to save them. But she could save her brothers. And she would, no matter what it took. Maybe some of her pain would then go away, some of her guilt. After that she would never look back.

Chapter Eight

Ellie paced the worn, wood floor of the house where she'd grown up. Her patience was wearing thin, and time was running out.

"Think of what you could do with that much money, Brett. You could buy a nice house in Tulsa and go to college," she tried telling him for the tenth time since arriving at the ranch.

Brett shook his head, his mouth drawn down in an uncharacteristic frown. "I want to ranch, not go to school."

"You and Matt never do anything, never go anywhere," she argued. "Just like Mama and Daddy."

"We're not livin' the folks' lives, Ellie," Brett said, his voice harsh and determined. "Matt and I do get out. You've just never been around enough to notice. You've led a glamorous life on the circuit, travelin' all over the country. You don't know the simple pleasures that we do."

And she didn't want to. "Rodeoing isn't that easy, Brett. And it sure isn't glamorous. It's a hard life."

"If it's so hard, why do you keep doin' it?"

"It's been bringing in money, hasn't it?" She'd reached the end of her rope, but the look of wounded pride on his face gave her nothing but misery. "I'm sorry. I shouldn't have said that. And this is my last year, anyway."

"Now you're really talkin' crazy," Brett muttered, and crossed the old-fashioned living room to plant himself on the sofa.

"I don't want to barrel race anymore, Brett. It's as simple as that."

"Now look who's being stubborn," Matt told her from the other side of the room. "You're the one with a streak a mile—" He stopped at the sound of a horn and walked to the window to look out. "Who the hell is that?"

Peering around him to see the late-model sedan coming to a stop in the ranch yard, she swallowed hard. "It's J.R."

Matt scowled at her. "You don't mean that real estate guy."

"Yes," she answered with a sinking heart. She'd told J.R. she'd have her brothers wrapped around her finger and ready to sign before she left for Las Vegas. She was two days from needing to leave, and she wasn't any closer to having them agree to sign than she had been before.

"Get him off my land," Matt growled.

"It's my land, too," Ellie reminded him.

"Two against one. Brett doesn't want him here, either."

She was desperate. She'd run out of time. "All you have to do to get rid of him is sign the papers."

Matt spun around, nearly knocking her over. "You're nuts, you know that, Ellie? I've a good mind to tell—"

"Matt!"

He glanced over his shoulder at Brett, who shook his head. Matt scowled at her. "Get him outa here."

When he'd stomped from the room, she turned to Brett. "I need to speak to J.R. privately."

With a shrug, he stood and walked to the door. "Be my guest. Just make it clear. We're not sellin'."

Her heart lodged in her throat when Brett brushed roughly past J.R. on the porch with no more than a glance. She was in trouble. Big trouble.

"Your brother doesn't look pleased to see me," J.R. remarked, stepping through the door she held open for him.

"I'm glad you're here. I need to talk to you." She waved him toward the sofa and waited for him to make himself comfortable, but she remained standing. There was nothing left to do but be honest. "I might as well tell you right off, Brett and Matt refuse to sign the papers releasing the ranch."

J.R. nodded. "I thought as much when you hadn't called me. What do you plan to do?"

Plan? Her plans were crashing around her like a house of cards. She'd been so sure she could make them see reason, she hadn't thought any further. "I don't know," she admitted.

J.R. stood and crossed the room to stand in front of her, then he circled her waist with one hand. Her ears thundered as he slowly pulled her closer. This wasn't the way she felt when Chace held her. Far from it. Her heart pounded now in fear and apprehension, not need and anticipation.

"I know what it is that you want," he said. "A house in the city. I can give you that."

"H-how?" she whispered, feeling suddenly light-headed.

"Marry me."

The room tilted. "Wh-what?"

He smiled, but it didn't warm her the way Chace's grin did. "I know I've taken you by surprise, and you have other things on your mind. Your brothers, for instance. I can help you with them. With the ranch."

"You'd do that?" she asked, surprised that he understood.

"That's what family is for, isn't it? To share?"

She couldn't believe this was happening. "Are you saying you…love me?"

He didn't speak for a moment. "I care for you, Ellie. Love will come later."

His face swam in her vision. She couldn't speak, couldn't think, couldn't breathe. None of this was real. It couldn't be.

Before she could gather her wits enough to think, he went on. "I'd like to be in Vegas with you for Finals, but business keeps me tied here. I can be there later, though. Vegas is the place for weddings. We can have ours there when you've finished competing."

His words barely registered as she thought about what he was offering. He could help her with her brothers, give her everything she'd planned for since that cold dark night at the creek. But was it what she truly wanted? Chace's words came back to her. *Be careful what you wish for.* But he couldn't have known. And she shouldn't be thinking of him.

Taking a breath, she tried to smile. "I don't know what to say."

"I'll meet you in Las Vegas on the last day of Finals. We'll see the sights, the shows, the casinos." His eyes glittered with anticipation. "And we'll find a nice chapel."

His chaste kiss left her cold, and the chill didn't leave her. Could she do this? A marriage of convenience? The idea was abhorrent, but if it helped her brothers, maybe it would make up some for not saving their parents.

When J.R. had gone, Ellie stood at the window, watching the trail of dust from his car when her brothers walked in. She didn't need to turn around to know Matt approached her.

"What's wrong, Ellie?"

"How could anything be wrong?" she said in a quiet voice. "J.R. just proposed."

"Marriage?" Matt thundered.

"Damn, Chace, you've been mopin' 'round here like a whipped dog," Trey said.

Chace placed the last of his rodeo shirts in the suitcase and closed it. "You're imagining things, baby brother."

"Sure. Me and my wild imagination. You haven't even argued with me about the dude ranch."

"Why should I?" Chace looked up from his packing. "You've gone and built the guest cabins." Shaking his head, he strode across the room to retrieve his shaving kit.

"So you'll come back and help me get things going?"

Chace saw the expectancy in his brother's eyes and shrugged. "Might as well. Nothin' else to do."

Trey ducked his head, grinning, and kicked at the handmade rug on the polished wood floor. "Shoot. Must be a woman that's got you so surly."

Giving him a sharp glance, Chace walked past him. "You're imagining things again."

The shrill ring of a phone cut off anything else Trey might have to say on the subject. Chace thanked his lucky stars for the interruption as he reached for his cell phone. "Brannigan," he barked into it.

"Chace, it's Matt Warren. We got trouble."

The all-too-familiar knot in his gut tightened. "What's going on, Matt?"

"It's that damned J.R."

"You haven't signed those papers, have you?" Chace glanced at his brother, who stood watching him with interest. Covering the mouthpiece, he quickly explained, "Jimmy Bob's at it again."

Matt sighed on the other end. "I wish to hell that's all this was about. It's bad, Chace. We gotta do something."

Fear gripped him. "Tell me," he demanded. "Is she okay?" He saw Trey's eyebrows shoot up and knew he'd have some explaining to do. "Has something happened to her?"

"Oh, something's happened all right," Matt said as if he were choking. "She's gonna marry him, Chace."

"Marry him?" Chace boomed into the phone. The room gave a strange lurch, and he sank onto the edge of the bed before his legs gave out. "What's going on? When?"

"After Finals. In Las Vegas. Brett and I tried talkin' to her, but she's a damn stubborn woman. Won't listen to anything we have to say. 'Course, I shoulda known she'd be this way. We wouldn't listen to her about the ranch.''

"You had that right. Ellie's being…" Crazy. Insane. *Desperate.* "I'm leaving in about an hour. Where will she be staying? In her camper?"

"No, she's taking her rig, but she's got a hotel room reserved. I don't know where, though. Brett and I would go, too, but we've got vaccinations. And Chace—there is oil.''

The news didn't surprise Chace. "Okay, thanks for letting me know. I'll track her down in Vegas and hopefully talk some sense into her,'' he promised before he ended the call. If nothing else, he would somehow get her to postpone a wedding until he could put a stop to J.R.'s scheme.

"Her? She?" Trey said with a mischievous grin. "What's this? I hear 'female and woman,' all the way.''

Chace stuffed the phone into his equipment bag and grabbed his suitcase. "My *woman* is marrying our worst enemy.''

Ellie dismounted and pressed her face into Sky Dancer's neck. "It's my fault,'' she whispered. "My mind wasn't on that race. We'll do better next time.''

Tugging her horse behind her, she tried to pinpoint what had her feeling so low. Matt and Brett didn't know she hadn't accepted J.R.'s proposal. They'd ranted and raved at first, but hadn't asked questions except for when the wedding was to take place. She'd told them as little as possible, and neither of them had commented. She took it as a good sign. Maybe they'd finally learned they couldn't tell her what to do.

She knew J.R. didn't love her. It eased her conscience to know she wouldn't be marrying him for love, either. Whatever his reasons, she'd make certain her brothers were safe. But even so, could she go through with it?

As she pushed through the other rodeoers gathered in the Thomas and Mack Center, the way opened up for her. She froze. Not ten feet away Chace stood propped against a stock rack, his arms folded on his chest and one boot crossed over the other. With his hat pulled low, she couldn't read the expression in his eyes, but she did see his slow smile. Her relief should have surprised her, but it didn't.

He shoved away from the fence and strolled over to her. "Guess you made it here okay," he said, stopping squarely in front of her.

"Chace. I...I didn't expect to see you." It wasn't completely true, but she hadn't known how she'd handle it when she did.

He tipped his hat back to look at her. "I saw your ride."

She made a face and looked down to stare at the dusty toes of her boots, embarrassed that he'd watched the worst she'd ridden since her early years in barrel racing. "Yeah, pretty bad, wasn't it?"

"It's just nerves, hon. It's a new arena for you. All the excitement, that's all. It'll get easier."

"I hope you're right." Looking up at him, she saw the concern in his eyes. It was the one thing she couldn't deal with. If it weren't for that, she might be able to walk away from him without a backward glance. But she wouldn't have to think about it much longer. Once she was out of rodeo, she wouldn't be running into Chace Brannigan. He'd be on his ranch in Texas, and she'd be— She didn't know. She ached to ask him to help her, but he didn't understand her need to get away from the ranch. Besides, she'd asked for his help once, and he'd turned her down. She wouldn't make that mistake twice.

"Any special plans for the week?" he asked.

She couldn't tell him about J.R.'s proposal. It had always been obvious that Chace didn't like the man. "Nothing special," she answered with a shrug, hating how close it was to a lie. "I guess I'll see the sights, rest and do my best, since this is my last rodeo."

Chace simply nodded, but she noticed the tight line of his lips and the hard glitter in his eyes.

"What about you?"

His gaze never left her face, as if he was waiting for her to say something. "The same, I guess. You planning to hang around for a while?"

Her heart leaped with hope that he'd suggest they spend some time together. But it quickly settled again when she remembered it would more than likely be the last time, whether she married J.R. or not. "I'll be here to watch you ride later."

An unidentifiable shadow crossed his face. "I came to wish you luck," he said, moving closer, "but that isn't all. There's something else—"

"Ellie," a voice behind her called.

She looked back to see J.R. moving toward them through the people and horses milling around. The sight of him caught her so much by surprise, she couldn't smother her gasp.

Chace's fingers wrapped around her arm, and he turned her back to him. "Ellie, we need to talk." He looked up quickly and then at her again. "But not here."

"I'm staying at the World Trade Hotel, room 321," she said as she glanced over her shoulder. The scowl on J.R.'s face made her nervous. What was he doing here so soon? She didn't want him saying anything to Chace about the possibility of a marriage. There wasn't any reason, until she made up her mind.

"I have to go," she said, pulling away from Chace.

"Wait. You can't— Aw, hell." He released her and backed away.

J.R. took her other arm. "There you are. I've been looking everywhere for you."

Her attention shifted to the man she could soon be marrying. "What are you doing here so early?" she asked, unable to keep the exasperation from her voice. "I didn't think you'd be here until later in the week."

J.R. released her with a smile. "It wouldn't be right to miss my fiancée's last rodeo. And I wanted to spend some time with my bride-to-be before the wedding."

Smothering her groan, she checked to see if Chace had heard. But he was gone. Through the mob of people, she could see his back. He was far enough away that he couldn't have heard. She'd have to talk to him later, although she didn't know what she'd tell him. Right now, she had to deal with J.R.'s unexpected arrival.

She glanced at her watch. "Where are you staying?" she asked, buying time before Chace's ride.

"The Mirage, but I haven't checked in yet. I came straight from the airport to see you."

She nearly sighed with relief. "Why don't you go check in, and I'll meet you there?"

He looked off in the direction Chace had gone, then steered her in the opposite one. "I'd rather drive you myself. I rented a car so you wouldn't have to drive your...truck.''

She didn't miss the note of distaste in his voice, as if *truck* were a dirty word. She couldn't deny that her beat-up old Chevy had seen better days, but why should he care? ''I guess I could use a new rig.''

''You won't need a truck and trailer in the city.''

The remark hit her like a slap in the face. ''I'm not giving up my horse.''

Placing his hand on the small of her back, he eased her along to the exit. ''Of course not. I'll have it boarded somewhere. The city is no place for an animal that size. And you'll be too busy with other things to do much riding.''

''But—''

''I'll pick you up in an hour. We'll see some of the city,'' he continued. ''It may be late when you get back to your hotel, so I'd rather you weren't driving alone.''

She nearly choked. She'd been traveling the country alone for years, and she wouldn't put up with any overprotective and antiquated ideas, if she agreed to marry him.

Before she had a chance to explain that she wouldn't be up to touring the gambling capital of the country later on that night, he'd kissed her cheek and left her with a smile that still didn't reach his eyes.

She watched him walk away, deciding she would have to let him know that she'd be a barrel racer until National Finals were over. After that—

She suddenly realized just how much she would miss about her life if she went to the city.

Holding back a wave of melancholy that threatened to overcome her, Ellie headed to tend to Sky Dancer.

Her encounter with J.R. didn't endear him to her, but she had to remember that she was considering his proposal for her brothers' sake. Only that thought kept her from running after him to tell him she didn't need his offer.

Chace chose a place where he had a clear view of the entire casino. From his seat he could see all the comings and goings in Caesar's Palace. One particular gambler, who, at that moment was laughing at something the brunette at his side was saying, held his attention.

The casino was crowded with people, the majority of them cowboys and their ladies. It was Sunday night, National Finals were over and everyone was trying to cram in all the enjoyment they could before they left for home at the end of the ten-day rodeo. But Ellie wasn't among the crowd.

Where was she?

The fact that he'd won both the saddle bronc championship and All-Around Cowboy title wasn't nearly as important to Chace as locating Ellie. It had been nothing but dumb luck that he'd known where to find her tonight. He hadn't seen more than a glimpse of her all week. He didn't know what had come over her, but her riding had improved since the first round. For the past nine days, she'd had a look of determination on her face that should've been a warning to her competition. She'd ridden Sky Dancer like he'd never seen her ride before. And he'd been proud.

But he hadn't been within fifty feet of her. If it hadn't been for Ray overhearing where she and J.R. planned to go for the evening, he would still be chasing around looking for them.

He was paying the waitress for his drink when J.R. walked away from the roulette table. Chace quickly made his way into the casino proper and placed himself in the man's path.

J.R.'s mouth twisted into the semblance of a smile. "Well, well. If it isn't my neighbor. Let me guess why you're here."

"Former neighbor," Chace reminded him. "You sold out to us."

"It was my mother who sold, not me." He flicked a piece of lint from his lapel, then pinned Chace with a glare. "If you're here to talk about Ellie and how you plan to tell her about what you refer to as my sordid past, you're wasting your time. This doesn't have anything to do with that."

Cold, hard, brown eyes dared Chace to refute it, but he didn't intend to beat around the bush. "Don't try conning me, Jimmy Bob. It won't work. I'm here for two things. First, I'm curious about why you're so desperate for the Warren ranch."

Shrugging, J.R. gave an unconcerned sniff. "Did it ever occur to you that it isn't about the land?"

"Bull."

"Ellie's a mighty fine little woman."

Chace fought to keep his temper. "I already know how fine she is, and I don't want anything to happen to her."

J.R.'s smile widened as he leveled his gaze at Chace. "You don't like me getting the woman you want. But I am."

"I figure it has to be money," Chace said, ignoring the dig. "I'll find out, and when I do—"

"And then you'll tell her how bad I am, right?" J.R. shook his head, and his smile disappeared. "She won't believe you. She believes I'm helping her. She wants off that ranch too much. I couldn't convince my mother not to sell out to the Brannigans, but I've convinced Ellie to marry me.''

J.R.'s words were like a punch, but Chace didn't let the impact stop him. ''She'll come to her senses and put two and two together.'' At least, he hoped she would.

''I can give her what she wants. A big house in the city, a husband with money—''

''*Her* money, I'm sure.''

''—and children,'' J.R. finished.

Chace balled his hands into fists. The thought of Ellie and J.R. together made him want to reach out and grab the man by his expensive silk tie.

''Face it, Chace. The Triple B won't last much longer. I've been in the same situation, only I didn't have oil to keep me in money. Cattle prices are down and feed prices are up. You can't take another year like the last five. I figure another six months and you'll be selling it.''

''The Triple B will never be for sale.''

''You're getting too old to keep earning enough money riding rough stock.''

''And yours is dirty.'' Chace took a deep breath and lowered his voice. ''The second thing is—you hurt Ellie and you won't be walking away. If you're not behind bars, you won't be walking anywhere. That's a promise.''

''Empty threats. You have nothing on me. I've done nothing illegal.''

''Only unethical, right?'' Chace let a smile ease over his face. ''I'm not the dumb cowboy I was when I left the ranch. If you want to find out how much I've learned in the past seventeen years, I'll be happy to teach you.''

J.R.'s eyes gleamed with challenge. "And I'll be teaching Ellie a few things.''

Knowing better than to rise to the bait, Chace gritted his teeth and broadened his smile. "Guess we'll see about that. I don't make promises I can't keep. You might want to remember that.''

Without waiting for a response, he turned and walked away. His suspicions were confirmed. The marriage had as much to do with Ellie and getting even for the loss of Staton land as it had to do with her ranch and her oil.

As he turned the corner to head for the door and some fresh air, he saw her standing alone, searching the gambling tables. He approached her from behind and, taking her arm, he silently led her through the crowd, away from the tables. Once they were out of J.R.'s vicinity, he let go of her and tucked his hands into his back pockets to keep from touching her again. This was his last chance to talk her out of making a serious mistake. He didn't have time to waste, although it was all he could do not to reach out and pull her into his arms. He had to put a stop to this crazy notion of hers and tell her the truth.

"Ellie, you don't have to do this.''

Ellie's heart leaped into her throat. Looking around, she silently prayed for a way to escape. "What are you talking about?''

"I know about your wedding plans.''

She wasn't able to stop the gasp that escaped her. How had he found out? Who would have told— Her brothers. When would they stop interfering in her life?

And when would Chace? Why wouldn't he just give up and let her do what she had to do?

"Don't start, Chace."

"It's time we had a talk, Ellie."

Wishing he'd go away and leave her alone, she squeezed her eyes shut and counted to five before opening them to glare at him. "I don't have anything to say."

"I do." He moved her farther away from the main part of the room and pointed to an empty sofa, his face stern. "Sit down."

Instead of obeying, she moved away. "Did it ever occur to you that I don't want to hear what you have to say?"

"Too bad."

"I don't have to listen to this." She spun on her heel, ready to flee, but he stopped her, wrapping his fingers around her wrist.

"This is a real sad way to get back at your brothers, Ellie."

"It's not payback, Chace," she answered, exasperated. "It's saving their lives and getting on with my own, in spite of what you think."

"It's ruining your life," he countered.

She desperately wanted to put her hands over her ears. He was wrong. He had to be. "That's your opinion."

Bright red flooded his face, and he threw up his hands, then dropped them to his side. "Dammit, Ellie, you can't do this."

She saw the muscle of his clenched jaw jump and reacted without thinking. A half step brought her nearer, and she pressed her palm to his cheek, hoping to calm him. "Don't you see? I can help them."

He relaxed at her touch and placed his hand over hers. "According to Matt, the ranch is doing okay. And it'll get better."

"Will it?"

He paused, and indecision flashed in his eyes. "Look, Ellie, there's—"

"You've never understood that I only want the best for my brothers. I don't want to see them give their lives to the ranch like our parents did. What guarantee is there that, even if the ranch does better, something won't happen to one of them?"

He wrapped his fingers around her hand and held it tightly. "Let go of it, Ellie. That was a long time ago. It was an accident. There was nothing you could do."

"I should have—" Tears threatened, and she shook her head to hold them back. "The ranch killed them. They gave their lives for it."

"You don't have to do the same."

Unwilling to hear more, she took a step back and eased her hand from his. "What do you mean? I'm doing what I've always wanted. I'm leaving the ranch. And not to live like some gypsy in a beat-up camper. The boys can stay, if that's what they want. I can't do anything about that, but I'll be able to help financially if anything goes wrong."

His eyes blazed with intensity as his voice lowered. "Do you think sacrificing yourself will bring your parents back?"

"No, of course not. Please understand. I'm not sacrificing myself," she insisted, stung by the harshness of his words. But his question unsettled her. If she listened to him any longer, she'd begin to believe he was right. He couldn't be.

As if he sensed her weakening, he went on. "You're jumping into something you're going to regret."

"You can't stop me, Chace," she said, hoping her voice sounded stronger than she felt. "Not even you and my brothers together. So get used to it."

When she started to turn away, he gripped her shoulders and brought her to a halt. "You don't need J.R. When the wells go in—"

Her breath caught on a gasp, and she stared at him. "Wells? What wells? What are you talking about?"

He broke the gaze, shaking his head, but he didn't release her. Looking at her again, his blue eyes locked with hers. "Oil wells, Ellie. There's oil on the ranch."

She remembered years before when an oil company had drilled test wells on the ranch. She'd been a child, but she'd heard the whispered conversations between her parents—all the what ifs. But there'd been no oil then, just as there wasn't now. She couldn't believe Chace would try something so desperate.

Slowly she pulled out of his grip and sighed. "Give it up, Chace."

Before she could turn away, he grabbed her arm, his fingers like a vise and his voice insistent. "Listen to me, Ellie. You don't—"

"Let go, Chace." With her free hand she pried his fingers from her upper arm. "I can't believe you'd lie to me."

Unable to keep from touching her, Chace placed his hands on her shoulders and looked down into her dark eyes. Sparks of angry gold glittered back at him. "Just listen to me. And trust me. Have I ever lied to you?"

"I don't know. Have you? Is keeping things from someone the same as lying?"

His throat tightened, and he had to swallow before he could speak. "What have I kept from you?"

The anger in her eyes was replaced with pain. "The fact that not only are you a rodeoer but a rancher, too. If I'd known that, I—" She shook her head and looked away.

"What? You what, Ellie?" He needed to know what she'd started to say. That she never would have had anything to do with him? That she never would have kissed him? She never would have—what? "Tell me."

She lowered her head, and when she answered, her voice was unsteady. "I thought we were friends, Chace. Maybe if you'd tell me why you don't like J.R., I could understand why you're doing this."

When she lifted her gaze to meet his, there was hope in her eyes, and he wanted to tell her everything. About how Jimmy Bob Staton had blamed the Brannigans for everything that had gone wrong in his life, when in truth, it was his own greed.

But if Ellie didn't believe him about the oil, she wouldn't believe him about this. "I can't," he said, his voice ragged.

She took a deep breath and straightened her shoulders beneath his hands. Her gaze moved past him before she spoke. "You know, Chace, it's really none of your business what I do."

The words were like a knife, cutting to the truth and stealing the little hope he had left. Releasing her, he dropped his hands to his side and took a step back. "Yeah, I know."

She straightened her hat and turned away.

"Ellie, what are you going to do?"

When she faced him again, her smile was bright,

but the light in her eyes was gone. "J.R. is going to show me how to play blackjack. Isn't this something? All the lights, the people, the money. I've never seen anything like it."

Before he could answer, J.R. appeared at her side. Ellie looked up at her fiancé with a smile. "I was just telling Chace you were going to teach me to gamble."

J.R. returned her smile, then directed it at Chace. Victory shined in his eyes. "Yes, I think she'll enjoy it. Goodbye, Chace."

Slipping away from J.R., she laid her hand on Chace's arm. "Good luck, Chace. Don't worry about me, okay?"

"Wish it were that easy." How he wished it were! He bent down and pressed his lips to hers, not caring what J.R. might do.

Chace watched Ellie walk away with J.R., the empty feeling inside him growing bigger. How could he let her go to him? How could he not?

Chapter Nine

Ellie's body trembled as J.R. led her through the casino. Oblivious to the crowd around them, she stared straight ahead. If she could hold on until later, when she was alone, she wouldn't cry. She just wouldn't think about Chace.

"What did he want?" J.R. asked.

"Nothing. Can we leave?" She'd had enough. A ten-day whirlwind tour of Europe couldn't have exhausted her more. She could have handled it, except for the nights after the rodeo waiting in the casinos. If this was the way J.R. expected her to live once they were married...

"I'll take you back to your hotel, and you can change."

Ellie came to a halt in the middle of the casino lobby. "Change?"

Beside her, he stopped, his mouth curved up in a smile. "Yes, for our wedding. I've found a chapel you'll like. Unless you want to be married by Elvis."

Unable to believe she'd heard him correctly, Ellie shook her head. She hadn't told him she'd marry him. She was tired and not thinking clearly, and she was no longer sure that marrying him was the right thing to do. "Not tonight, J.R. I need to get some sleep."

His arm tightened around her waist as he led her to the door. "We've put it off long enough."

Resisting his efforts, she pulled away. He couldn't force her to do something she'd been having major doubts about. "No. I want some questions answered first."

"We'll talk later."

Ellie relented for the moment and let him lead her out into the Nevada night. She didn't want to cause a scene in public, and she needed a few minutes to regain the control J.R. had taken from her. How had she allowed that to happen?

They waited for the rental car and when it pulled up, the valet jumped out to rush around and open the door for her. Ellie slid inside and watched J.R. leave the young man a large tip before getting behind the wheel.

She sorted through her jumbled thoughts and remained silent while he maneuvered through the traffic along the glitter of the Strip. The more time she spent with J.R., the more she wondered what he would gain from a marriage to her. She had nothing to offer. He didn't love her any more than she loved him. She only wanted the assurance that her brothers and their ranch would be safe. He could give her that. But what would she be giving him?

When the car came to a stop in front of her hotel, J.R. draped his arm along the back of the seat and studied her. "I'll be back for you in an hour. Be sure to bring some identification. That's all we'll need."

Panic squeezed at her heart. It had been two weeks since he'd proposed, and she hadn't felt right since then. She needed more time to think before she went through with this. "I thought it was bad luck for the bride and groom to see each other before the ceremony," she said, stalling.

"Usually I'd agree. But this marriage isn't 'usual,' is it? We both know you're marrying me for my money." When she stiffened and moved closer to the door, he reached across the small space separating them and ran a finger down her arm. "It doesn't bother me. People do it every day."

She fought off a shiver. "The money isn't for me," she said in defense. "It's for the ranch. For Matt and Brett."

"Of course. There'll be plenty of money for them, too."

But would there? She'd seen J.R. gamble every night, winning money, losing it, then winning it back again. For her, life was enough of a gamble. What would happen to her brothers if he gambled his money away?

"J.R.?"

He peered at her in the dark interior of the car, his brows drawn together in a frown. "What is it?"

"How lucrative is the real estate business?"

"In this case, very lucrative."

The statement sent chills through her. "What does that mean?"

"Will you stop asking questions?" he snapped. With a sigh he pulled back. "I'm sorry. Don't worry about it. Once we're married, everything will be taken care of."

The chills intensified. Her brothers didn't like the man. Reba, her dearest friend, had always been suspicious. And Chace's announcement of oil on the ranch shouted in her memory. If she went ahead with this, she'd be marrying a man she barely knew, against the advice of everyone who cared about her.

Warning bells went off in her mind. Could Chace have been telling her the truth? After all, she'd spent so many years in rodeo, oil testing might have advanced the same way other technology had. If J.R. knew there was oil on the ranch, by marrying her, *he* would be the one to gain.

"What are you getting out of this marriage, J.R.?"

He took a deep breath and let it out, clearly announcing his impatience. "Don't worry about me. I'll be getting just what I want."

When he leaned closer to her, she held up her hand to stop him. "Is there oil on the ranch? Is that it?"

His eyes narrowed, giving him a sinister look. "What did that meddling Brannigan tell you?"

Something in the way he said the name Brannigan sent another wave of chills through her. "It's you. Your family feuded with his for four generations."

"What difference does it make?" J.R. snarled. "You need me too much to back out now."

Her mind cleared when he started the car, and she knew what she had to do. Grabbing the door handle, she threw open the door and scrambled out. "You're wrong. So very wrong."

"Get back in here!"

But she wasn't about to stay in the car with him another second. Without even a glance over her shoulder, she hurried into the hotel. Luckily an elevator was waiting, and she bolted into it, punching her floor button with a shaking finger.

When the doors slid open again, she ran for her room. She felt safer once she reached it, but her hands fumbled with her key card at the lock. Down the hall she heard the elevator doors slide open.

"Ellie!" J.R. shouted.

She dropped her card and bent to retrieve it, her heart pounding. She didn't know what he might do if she didn't get into her room. Straightening again, she saw him coming toward her.

"Chace was right," she called to him. "I never should have trusted you. What a fool I've been. I'm not after your money. You're after mine."

He grew nearer, his fists balled. "You can't prove that."

"I will if I have to," she answered, shoving the card into the lock. "I will, if you don't leave here now." She turned the knob and opened the door to slip inside. Slamming the door as he reached it, she flipped the security lock with trembling fingers. Knees weak, she leaned against the door.

"Open the door," he said through the barrier. "We can talk about this. We can work out some kind of arrangement. Whatever you want."

She flattened her hands on the door and leaned her forehead against it, praying he'd go away. "Not on your life. It's over, J.R. You'd better get out of Vegas. You'd better hide, because when I tell Chace—"

"Chace can't help you. I—"

Covering her ears with her hands to keep from hearing any more, she moved across the room in the dark. When her knee connected with the bed, she sank down onto it. Her body shook, and she could barely breathe. She'd come so close to making a terrible mistake. How could she have even considered marrying J.R.? The things he'd promised to do for her no longer mattered. What a fool she'd been for turning a deaf ear to the people who cared about her. Matt and Brett had warned her. Chace had—

Choking back a sob, she buried her face in her hands. She couldn't think about Chace. Not now. Not when her life was crashing around her. There were other things to figure out. How would she help her brothers? How would she live? Where would she go? Would she now be forced to return to the ranch?

When the pounding finally stopped she prayed J.R. had given up and gone away. She tried to concentrate on a plan for her future, but she couldn't hold back thoughts of Chace for long. Memories tiptoed into her mind until sensations poured through her. She'd spent her life building walls to keep from getting hurt. To stay strong. She'd made plans to keep from losing those she loved.

And then she'd met Chace. Every time he looked at her, every time he touched her, he tore down a little more of her defenses. How would she go on without Chace in her life?

She couldn't deny she loved him, and he'd never said he loved her, but when he kissed her... If only she could tell him how she felt. But what did she know about something like that? And when would she get the chance?

She didn't know how long she'd been sitting in the dark when she heard a knock on her door. When the knocking grew to pounding, her patience slipped. ''Maybe he'll understand rude,'' she muttered on her way to the door. She reached it and took a deep breath, prepared to say whatever it would take to get J.R. to leave her alone. But before she could say the words, she was stopped by the voice on the other side.

"Hey, Ellie."

Chace had to lean against the door frame to keep from falling over after Ellie had undone the locks and flung open the door. She looked awful. And still he wanted her.

He'd known since the first time he'd laid eyes on her that she did things to him no other woman ever had. He'd chalked it up to wanting to protect her. And then he had blamed it on the challenge she presented. But neither was what kept him coming back.

He ached to take her in his arms, but he couldn't risk getting her riled and getting himself kicked out.

"You gonna invite me in?" he asked

She stared at him, her eyes wide and brown like a deer caught in headlights. "I—"

"Good." He shoved away from the door and stepped inside, but didn't go any farther. Beyond her the room was dark, except for the light shining from the hallway. She was still dressed in the same jeans and shimmery shirt she'd been wearing at the rodeo and in the casino, so he knew there'd been no wedding. Not yet, anyway. His gaze slid over her, taking in every detail, burning the vision into his memory.

Reaching beside the door, he felt for the light switch and flipped it on. A table lamp bathed her in a soft glow. He waited while she closed the door, unable to take his eyes off her, and noticed her hesitation. His gaze followed hers when she glanced in the direction of the bed.

"You had a bed in the camper, Ellie," he reminded her in a husky voice he couldn't control.

The shadows in the room played over her face, hiding her expression as she answered in a soft voice, "Yes, I guess I did."

He hadn't come to seduce her. He'd only come to see her one last time and wish her well. But his body wanted more, and even his mind was leading him down a path he didn't have any intention of following. Moving past him, her arm bumped his, and the small contact didn't help his physical state or his mental one. His resolve not to touch her weakened.

Glancing at him, she walked over to sit on the edge of the bed. She picked at the bedspread and kept her head lowered.

Dammit! He'd come to tell her goodbye, but once he said it, he would have to leave. And he couldn't do that. Not yet.

"Mind if I sit?" he asked.

She shook her head, and he made his way to a chair on the far side of the room. Thankful that he wasn't close to her, and cursing the distance at the same time, he wondered what he could say to keep him there until he could finally force himself to leave.

"How'd your month off go?" he asked, snagging the first thing he could think of. "Do any competing?"

She shook her head, and a smile softened her face. "I got in a little practice. And a group of school kids came out to the ranch to visit. It seems I'm a celebrity around home."

"Yep, it happens," he said, nodding, his tension easing a little. "I remember the first time I made it to National Finals. Makes a person feel like some kind of hero."

"There was one little girl. She lives in town and hasn't ever ridden a horse. I could see how much she wanted to ride, but she didn't say a word. I wanted to give her a ride, but I couldn't. If I had, the rest would have begged for one."

Her eyes shone with a light he'd never seen before. The joy on her face was almost more than he could handle. "Maybe you can give her one when you get back."

The sparkle in her eyes dimmed. "Maybe."

"Christmas vacation. That'd be a good time," he went on, hoping the mention of the holiday would bring back her smile.

"I— Yes, that's an idea. If I'm around."

Chace couldn't take any more. He'd done everything he could to stop her from ruining her life, but he had nothing that she wanted to give her.

Standing, he closed the distance between them and reached down to take her hands, drawing her to her feet. She offered no resistance when he wrapped his arms around her waist.

"Guess you haven't changed your mind about those plans of yours," he whispered.

Resting her head against his chest, she trembled. "I'm so sorry."

He closed his eyes, absorbing the feel of her pressed against him. She might say she didn't want him, yet every inch of her told him that she did. But nothing like the way he wanted her.

She pulled away enough to gaze up at him, her eyes dark in the dimly lit room. Touching the top snap of his shirt, she smiled. "I've always wondered..."

He swallowed, his breath lodging in his chest at the desire in her eyes. "What?" he croaked.

Slipping her fingers into the opening of his shirt, she popped the snap. Moving down, she unsnapped the next one. "Just...wondered."

"Damn, Ellie," he breathed.

She raised her eyebrows when she finished the job and spread his shirt wide, pressing her hands to his chest.

"Ellie. Hon?"

"Don't worry. I know what I'm doing."

He had no doubt she believed it, but as far as he was concerned she was killing him. He'd had no plans to seduce her, and he sure as hell hadn't expected her to seduce him. Even worse, he had to stop her.

Didn't he?

Closing his eyes against the onslaught of his traitorous body, he tried to form the words that would bring her seduction to a halt. After all, she was about to be married. He had to respect that even if he didn't like it.

"I can feel your heart beating," she whispered.

He looked down to see her undoing the buttons of her shirt. "Baby, don't—"

Her hand froze. "Am I doing something wrong?"

Wrong? She was doing everything right. With a deep groan he ducked his head and captured her lips, brushing his mouth over hers, drugging himself so he wouldn't have to think. He swept her into his arms, cradling her to him while he plunged the depths of her sweet mouth. Tasting her again drove away all thoughts of leaving; her response short-circuited the last of his control.

Placing her gently on the bed, he broke the kiss only long enough to slide his shirt off, then he lay down next to her. With fingers that shook, he unbuttoned the rest of her shirt. The sight of her lacy red bra made him catch his breath.

"Like it?" she asked in a smoky voice, her eyes matching the sound of it. "There's more."

He pressed his mouth to the top curve of a breast spilling over the top of the delicate lace, then he brushed a thumb across one taut nipple that strained at the nearly sheer fabric. The moan it pulled from her rocked him so deeply, he ached. His mouth came down on hers, punishing her for making him feel things he didn't want to feel, yet needing to feel it all. But he quickly gentled the kiss, afraid he would hurt her. Reining in the passion that threatened to consume him, he moved to place a kiss in the hollow between her breasts.

"Chace," she said in a breathy whisper that turned his insides to a ball of fire.

"Hmmmm?"

"I..."

He leaned back to look at her and found her dark lashes brushing her cheeks. Tipping her chin up, he forced her to open her eyes. "What is it, hon?"

"I—I've never—" She shook her head and avoided his gaze.

Watching her face, he wondered what she was trying to say. Suddenly he knew. He felt like someone had zapped him with a cattle prod. "You don't mean you're a— You've never—"

"Never." She glanced at him, then turned her head away. "You're disappointed."

"Disappointed?" Far from it. If this woman responded to him with the same fire while making love as she had already, he'd never live through it.

"I was saving myself," she whispered.

Reality hit him with a punch that left him breathless. He knew what she was getting at and the man she'd chosen for her husband, and it wasn't him. A low-down, no-good Staton didn't deserve to breathe the same air as this woman, yet she was marrying him. It would be the revenge of a lifetime to have her first.

But he couldn't do it and then let her walk out of his life and into the arms of another man. Once he'd loved her, he knew he couldn't let another man have her.

He groaned as he moved away. "Maybe you should stick to your plan," he said, leaving the bed to retrieve his shirt.

"You don't want me?"

"I wish I didn't," he murmured. Tugging on his shirt, he watched her breasts rise and fall with each breath. Bending over her, he pulled her shirt together, buttoning it for her as she lay on the bed, staring at him. He ached to touch her soft skin again, but he did it carefully, making sure he didn't even brush her skin with his fingers. When he finished, he backed away.

She turned her face away from him, and he felt a pain he'd never experienced before. "Look at me, Ellie."

She moved her head from side to side, biting her lip.

"Please."

The pain in his chest sharpened when he saw the tears glistening in her eyes. He took her hand and eased her to her feet. Holding her in his arms, he closed his eyes for a moment, savoring the feel of her body next to his for the last time. He moved his hands to cradle her face and looked into her dark eyes. "I want you to be happy."

"But, Chace—"

He pressed his lips to hers before releasing her. "If you need me, I'll be at the Triple B."

"You're going?" she asked as he walked to the door.

He turned for one last look. "Yeah," he said, forcing a laugh that sounded more like a coyote in a trap. "To a dude ranch."

Ellie packed, smoothing the rough denim of her jeans and the slippery satin of her Western shirts, as different as the feel of Chace's skin and hers. Cursing herself, she brushed at a wayward tear with the back of her hand before snapping the locks on her old suitcase. She hadn't cried since the day her parents had been lowered into the ground, and she wasn't about to do it again. Sorrow had brought her tears that long-ago day—a deep sorrow and emptiness that had taken years to overcome. Chace had done a lot to help her fill the void, even when she'd done her best to turn him away. In time she knew she'd heal, even from her guilt.

But he'd refused her offer. He didn't want her. He didn't love her. And she'd been a fool to think he might. She couldn't face him again, knowing how inexperienced and inept she must have appeared. Now everything in her life lay in a heap of ashes at her feet.

But even though she kept telling herself she didn't care, or at least soon wouldn't, she couldn't stop wishing things were different. At least she'd learned a lesson. Matt and Brett were grown men. If she resented the way they tended to overprotect her at times, she'd done the same to them. She'd tried to force them into living their lives the way she thought was best for them, as though they hadn't done a good job with the ranch these past few years. Her guilt had been a driving force. Someday she'd find a way to make it up to them.

She'd ridden the ride of her life in the tenth and final round, placing second for the day and finishing in sixth place in the National Finals Rodeo Barrel Racing. But she didn't feel the joy she would have expected. She didn't feel anything.

Even knowing that Chace had captured both the Saddle Bronc Championship and the coveted title of Best All Around Cowboy didn't cheer her.

She'd been a fool to think he felt more than friendship for her. Worse yet, and the reason she had to continue blinking away the moisture that formed at the thought of what she'd done, she'd offered herself, body and soul, to him. And he'd refused.

With a hard shake of her head to chase away the memories, Ellie gathered her things and started for the lobby desk. The elevator ride gave her the chance to pull herself together. There'd be time enough for self-pity and recriminations on the drive—

Home. The word came to mind as the elevator doors opened, and she realized she had nowhere else to go. Crossing the empty lobby, she squared her shoulders, determined to at least get out of the hotel before she resorted to tears.

Placing her key card on the highly polished wood of the reservations counter, she pulled her checkbook from her tote bag. "I'd like to check out," she told the young desk clerk.

"Miss Warren?" he asked, after checking the computer in front of him.

Slipping a pen from its holder, she waited. "That's right. How much is it?"

He looked up from the screen. "Your bill has been taken care of."

Ellie opened her mouth to speak, then shut it. She blinked once, twice, then cleared her throat. "I'm sure you're mistaken."

"No, ma'am. The room and all amenities are paid in full."

J.R.

Her eyes narrowed. Who else could have done it? If he'd had his way, they'd be Mr. and Mrs. J. R. Staton.

She shook her head. He was the least of her problems. If she never saw him again it would be too soon. Too bad she couldn't say the same about Chace.

Chace.

He'd brought happiness into her life again. She hadn't realized how sheltered she'd been, even on the circuit. How naive she was. Then he'd stepped into her life and changed it. No matter how much she tried to tell herself otherwise, she couldn't imagine a life of happiness without him. She couldn't imagine a *life* without him. She'd been so self-sufficient for so long, she'd never felt she needed anyone. But she now realized that letting someone care meant letting them help. Loving them meant—

Loving them meant letting them go. That's what Chace had done. Hadn't he said he wished he didn't want her? She hadn't understood him then, but she did now. He knew he didn't fit into her plan. Her foolish plan. He thought she was marrying J.R.

She glanced at her watch. One o'clock. Maybe she could catch him.

Her request to use the phone brought another smile
from the young man behind the desk. With his assis-
tance she dialed the number to Chace's hotel. When
no one answered in his room, she tried the main desk
and learned he was no longer registered.

"He checked out?" she asked, her stomach churn-
ing. "When? What time?"

"I'll have to check," the woman on the other end
answered.

"Never mind," Ellie replied, hanging up. She
thanked the desk clerk and grabbed her luggage.

"I'll call a bellboy to help you," he said.

"I don't have time," she called over her shoulder.

In her truck, with Sky Dancer secure in the trailer,
Ellie left the lights of Vegas behind. For the first time
in years she didn't have a plan.

"Where is he?" she whispered to the diamond-
studded sky spread out ahead of her. As soon as the
question was out of her mouth, she knew the answer,
and a plan began to form. He'd told her he'd be there
if she ever needed him. And she needed him.

Chapter Ten

After leaving Ellie, Chace and Ray had stopped at the hotel bar where Chace had hoped to numb the ache that had only grown worse since he'd left Ellie in her hotel room. With two drinks under his belt, that had only made him think—and feel—more clearly, he had finally returned to her hotel and paid her bill. His wedding gift to her. At least he could give her something. The thought of J.R.'s face when he found out about it would have made Chace smile if he hadn't been so damn miserable. After that, he'd had a change of heart, and hoped the knot hadn't already been tied. But calls to every wedding chapel in the area had netted him nothing. They hadn't gotten married in Vegas, but that didn't mean they wouldn't. Whatever it took, he had to stop her.

Because he knew his trailer would slow him down, Chace awakened his old friend, Ned, who'd competed and done well in the bareback competition, and hired him to pull it back to the Triple B. Ray would ride along to his home in Colorado, then Ned would pull the trailer on to the Triple B. Ned was ready to retire, too, and Trey had been trying to talk the man into working at the Triple B. Not only would Chace be relieved of his horse and trailer, he'd be doing Trey a favor by delivering Ned to the ranch.

Driving away from Vegas, Chace checked the time, realizing he could be a good four hours or more behind Ellie and J.R. Even if he drove like a bat out of hell, he'd never catch up with them. He didn't know where they might be headed or which route they might be taking. He hoped it would be Tulsa, since that's where J.R.'s office was.

He'd planned to drive straight through, but after no sleep, he was forced to stop in Albuquerque. Even then, sleep didn't come easily. The few hours he managed to slip in rested him and, after a quick meal, he hit the road again. By the next morning he was fighting the Tulsa rush-hour traffic, muttering curses at the other drivers.

At J.R.'s office building, he strode past the empty receptionist's desk and through the open doorway into the real estate agent's inner office. "Where is she, Jimmy Bob?"

J.R.'s look of surprise was evident by his opened mouth. He closed it quickly, pasting a smile on his face and rising from behind his desk. "Must be planning our wedding."

Relief flooded Chace. "The wedding didn't take place."

"Give it up, Brannigan. I'll win this one, sooner or later."

"Over my dead body," Chace growled. "Or yours."

"I'm warning you, Brannigan—"

"No, I'm warning you, Staton." Chace moved to the desk where several boxes were stacked. "Where is she?"

J.R. scowled at him. "Why ask me? I haven't seen her since Sunday night after we left the casino."

Incredulous, Chace stared. Sunday night? *Before* he'd gone to her hotel room? If so, had she known she wasn't marrying J.R.? She hadn't said a word, but he hadn't given her the chance. If he'd known— The thought nearly brought him to his knees.

"She's all yours," J.R. said with a distorted smile. "I only wanted her ranch. And I'd have had it and the oil." He shook his head. "Just get out."

"Not before I find out one thing," Chace said, standing his ground. "Why'd you cut her alternator belt?"

"You get crazier all the time, Brannigan," J.R. replied, unbuttoning the top button of his shirt under his loosened tie.

Chace recognized the familiar nervous action and knew he had him. Before leaving Vegas, Ray had found a witness to J.R.'s activities in Phoenix. "You were seen at the campground on the morning her truck broke down."

J.R.'s eyes narrowed before he let out a long breath. "Okay," he said without looking Chace in the eye. "I thought if I could keep her from the next rodeo, she couldn't compete, so she couldn't earn enough money for Finals. If she didn't make it to Vegas, she would have to get her brothers to sign the sale contract. It was the only way she'd have the money to get away from the ranch."

"You ought to be whipped for doing that, Jimmy

Bob. But since I know you won't be bothering her again, I'll save it for another time."

"If you can find me," J.R. muttered.

Chace started for the door and his gaze took in the state of the room. He turned back. "Looks like you're packing it up. Law on your tail?"

J.R.'s jaw tightened. "No. I'm…relocating."

Chace saw the man's hands shake when he picked up a stack of papers, then glance nervously at the phone. "Gambling debts?"

When J.R.'s head jerked up at the words, Chace saw the answer in the fear in his eyes. "You'd better get your sorry hide as far from me as possible, Jimmy Bob, because if anybody comes around asking questions, I won't hesitate to tell them everything I know. And I know enough. If you want to gamble, put your money on not seeing Ellie again. That's a sure bet."

Leaving Tulsa, he knew there was only one place left to look for Ellie, but when he reached the Warren ranch, he learned she hadn't been there, either.

In his truck again, he leaned his head back against the seat. If J.R. and her brothers hadn't seen her, where the hell had she gone? He'd promised Trey he'd get back to the Triple B as soon as he could. They had work to do to get things ready. Ned would already be there with Redneck and his trailer. Chace hadn't told anybody where he was headed. Only that he'd get to the ranch as soon as he could. He'd expected to find Ellie and take her back with him, whether she was willing or not. He hadn't thought about what he'd do, once he had her there. He hadn't thought that far ahead. But it didn't matter much if he couldn't find her. He was lost with no clues as to where she'd disappeared.

* * *

After getting directions from a nearby town, Ellie drove down the long, winding drive through acres and acres of rocky rangeland, hoping she was doing the right thing. She didn't know what she would say to Chace when she arrived at the Triple B. She hoped he would let her explain. *If* she could think of an explanation that sounded rational. And maybe she would get some answers of her own.

At the top of the hill, she saw a two-story stone house that took her breath away. This was Chace's home? No wonder he wanted to come back. The mellowed stone gave off a warmth, even from a distance, beckoning to those who saw it. Slowing her pickup to a crawl, Ellie took in the expansive number of outbuildings and the row of what she decided must be guest cabins on the outskirts of a well-kept lawn. In the distance the land dropped away to an endlessly breathtaking view of the countryside.

She pulled up in front of a hand-hewn log fence and turned off the engine. It took several deep breaths to get her nerves under control enough to open the door and step out.

"You can do it," she muttered to herself on the way to the wide, welcoming porch. At the massive wooden door, she ran her fingers through her hair and licked her lips, then took another deep breath. She knocked and waited.

The door swung open, and she looked into a pair of eyes the same color as Chace's but not his. Stunned speechless by the resemblance, she forced her tongue from the roof of her mouth to speak. "Is, um, Chace around?"

"You've gotta be Ellie" came the answer as the

cowboy at the door looked her up and down. He added a grin that soothed the edges of her nerves.

"How do you figure that?" she asked.

He tossed back his head and laughed, throwing the door wider. "Welcome to the Triple B. Make yourself at home. And I sure do mean that."

"Chace isn't expecting me," she tried to explain, stepping into the cool, dark interior of an entry hall.

"Chace isn't here."

Disappointment squeezed her heart. "Oh. Well..."

"You bring your horse?"

"He's, um, in the trailer."

"I'll have Ned put your horse up and take care of your rig." He stuck his hands in his pockets and gave her a contagious grin. "By the way, I'm Trey."

"I figured that out," she told him with a smile, and stuck out her hand. "Chace talks about you a lot."

"Cussin' a blue streak, I'll bet." Trey took her hand in both of his, wrapping them in warmth.

"If he isn't here, I'll just head back home. My brothers will be wondering where I am."

Instead of letting her go, he pulled her arm through his and led her down the hallway. "Can't let you do that. You can give your brothers a call if they'll be worried. Chace'll be home anytime. If he heard I let you get away, he'd have my hide. We've got plenty of room here."

They stepped into a large kitchen with wooden beams and warm golden walls. A huge, round oak table took center stage on the flagstone floor. "Have a seat," he said, pointing to one of the chairs.

While he crossed the room to an oversize refrigerator and took out a pitcher of iced tea, she settled at the table and wondered how to get herself out of the awkward situation. "I don't know that he'll want to see me," she forced herself to say. "Last time I saw him—" The memory of how she'd offered herself to Chace brought heat to her face. "Let's just say things didn't go well."

His hands full of glasses he'd taken from a high cabinet, he turned to look at her. "You ditch Jimmy Bob?"

Ashamed that she'd even known the man and unable to say anything, she nodded.

"Chace'll be happy as heck to see you, then." He set the glasses on the table, retrieved the pitcher and poured the tea. Easing himself into a chair, he took a drink. "Sorry," he said with an apologetic smile. "Been ridin' fence."

"So you're still ranching?"

"Always be ranchin'. This'll be a workin' dude ranch. None of that phony stuff here. If it hadn't been for Chace and Dev sendin' money..." He shook his head and looked at her. "I know this isn't what Chace wants for the Triple B, but he's warming to the idea."

She smiled, remembering Chace's last words to her. "He's coming around."

Trey chuckled and pushed back his chair, finishing his tea in one long drink. "I'll take you upstairs and show you to a room. Chace oughta be here in the next day or two. Don't know where he got off to. Ned didn't have any idea, either. But he'll be home. Told me he would."

"Thank you," she said, and followed him. Now all she had to do was wait. And worry. And wonder what she was going to say to Chace when he returned.

Chace was sick of worrying, but he couldn't stop. Another ten hours of driving had brought him within

spitting distance of the Triple B, and he still didn't
have a clue where Ellie was. But he'd learned one
thing. He loved her. Plain and simple. Probably had
since the first time he'd seen her perched on the shovel
in her camper. Realizing it, though, had snuck up on
him.

He never stopped thinking about her during the day,
and at night he dreamed of her. Of making her happy
and easing her fears. Of holding her close and waking
up with her in the morning. Of loving her until they
were both left exhausted, only to start all over again.
She was smarter than he'd given her credit for. He
hadn't given her the chance to tell him she'd dumped
J.R. He should've known she wouldn't offer herself to
him, only to go off and marry J.R. afterward.

Damn! How could he have been so thick-headed?

In the ranch yard he turned off the truck ignition
and forced his weary body out of the cab. He was
tired, he was hot and he was mad as hell. Trey would
just have to understand when he left again. As soon
as he found Ellie, he'd find a way to keep the Triple
B going without being there. *If* he found Ellie. But *if*
wasn't a part of it. He'd find her.

Dragging his feet up the porch steps, he tried to
think of where he'd start. Tulsa, he guessed. That
would be the closest place. If she wasn't there, he'd
call Reba. Maybe Ellie had gotten in touch with her.
If Ellie was hiding from him— The thought didn't
bear thinking.

With a heavy sigh he threw open the front door.
"Trey! Trey, where are you?"

Startled, Ellie bolted straight up from the deep chair
where she sat reading a travel magazine. The sound

of the heavy front door slamming, followed by the thunder of boots hitting stone, brought her to her feet.

Chace. He sounded mad as a bear with his nose in a beehive.

The double doors to the room flew open with a bang, and she nearly jumped out of the chair.

Chace's eyes, narrowed by a scowl, searched the room, landing on her. His hand froze on his hat as he reached for it. "Ellie?"

"Hey, Brannigan," she answered, her nerves stretched to the limit.

He jerked his hat from his head, took two steps toward her, and stopped. "Where the hell have you been?"

"Here."

"Here? At the Triple B?"

She nodded.

Approaching her with long, strong strides, he tossed his hat to a nearby chair. "Dammit, Ellie, I've been hunting all over half the country for you. Why didn't you tell somebody you were coming here?" He scooped her into his arms, holding her close. "Matt and Brett are worried sick about you. And I'm half-crazy from wondering what happened."

"I called them and told them where I am and that I won't force them to sell the ranch. They haven't been that happy since their favorite bull won the Grand Championship at the fair," she explained, hoping to ease his mind.

Lifting a trembling hand to his cheek, she smoothed his hard jaw. She knew better than to read anything into his actions or his words. "Stop frowning, Chace. I'd much rather see you smile. Then I'd know if you're happy to see me or not."

"Happy?" He held her at eye level, his frown deepening. "I'm mad as hell that you've sent me running all over the place to find out that you've been here waiting for me. Ellie, I—"

"Trey and I have been talking," she rushed on. "I'm here to apply for the job of riding instructor at the Triple B Guest Ranch. If that's all right with you."

He stared at her before setting her on her feet. "Riding instructor? You came here for a job?"

She couldn't tell him the truth—that she couldn't bear the thought of a life without him. When Trey had talked about the dude ranch, her plan to apply for riding instructor had taken root. She would have the opportunity to meet new people—people who weren't from the world of rodeo. People from all over the country. And she'd be near Chace.

But he didn't look too happy with her explanation. She was afraid he would send her packing, and she hurried to add to it. "A job. Yes, I— Well, you see, what with not marrying J.R. and all— I thought that with my experience..." She shrugged, not knowing how to go on.

He crossed his arms on his chest. "On a ranch."

Nodding, she bit her lip. He didn't look convinced, but then a thought struck her. "Why were you looking for me?"

"When I found out you weren't marrying J.R., I thought my worries were over. But then I couldn't find you. I thought I'd go crazy."

Her heart took wing. "You missed me?"

"Missed you?" He pulled her into his arms, holding her captive. "Hell, Ellie, I love you. Heart and soul. I swear it. You're not leaving here. Not alone. Not as long as I'm alive. And if you try to, you'd better have a saddle made for two on Sky Dancer, 'cause I'll be going with you. We can live anywhere you want. Tulsa. Dallas. Even New York.''

Feeling faint with joy, she could barely speak. ''We?''

His smile touched her heart, and his eyes burned with determination. ''You're going to marry me.''

''Chace,'' she said on a giddy sigh, ''you're supposed to ask. Don't be so bossy.''

Going down on one knee, he held her hands and gazed up at her. ''Ellie Warren—''

''Elaine Susan Warren,'' she corrected.

His grin widened. ''*Elaine Susan* Warren, will you do me the honor of becoming Mrs. Chace *Aaron* Brannigan?''

She pressed her lips together, wanting to tell him yes, but two things stood in her way. ''Why didn't you tell me that J.R. was a part of the feud that had caused your family so much trouble?''

''Would you have believed me?''

''I wouldn't have had any reason not to.''

He placed a kiss in each palm. ''I wasn't sure what he was up to, and then I told you about the feud. I couldn't tell you more. I was afraid you'd think I was telling you it hadn't ended and you were a part of it.''

''Has it?''

Silent for a moment, he nodded. ''For now.''

That was good enough for her. She hoped they'd never see J. R. Staton again, but she knew there were no guarantees.

''Chace?''

His gaze met hers, and she could tell by the look in his eyes that he was waiting for her question. But she didn't know how to go about asking it.

Taking a deep breath, she tried. "Will you tell me why—that night at the hotel—why you didn't…"

He grabbed her around the waist and settled in the big chair, cradling her on his lap. His eyes darkened to a deep-blue as he looked at her. "Damn, Ellie. Don't you know how much I wanted you that night? Hell, I've had women throw themselves at me before, but it was nothing like what you were offering."

"But you didn't take me up on it," she whispered, burying her face in his chest and breathing in the scent of him. Horses, fresh air and Chace. All cowboy. And she loved him.

"I thought you were marrying J.R., I thought we had no future together," he explained, nuzzling her neck to send her heart racing. "If I'd taken you then, I couldn't have given you up. And I knew I had to."

"You loved me that much?"

"Enough to pay your hotel bill."

She looked up to see his blue eyes twinkling and she stared at him. "That was you? I thought—"

He stopped her with a kiss. "I loved you that much, but I didn't know. It took nearly losing you to make me see just how much."

"I thought I'd lost you, too," she told him, remembering the panic she'd felt, the utter desolation. "But we're here now. At the Triple B. Why didn't you tell me how beautiful it is?"

"You said you hated ranching. I want you to be happy, Ellie. Wherever you want to go, whatever you want to do, we'll do it together. I'll find something—"

She pressed her fingers to his lips. "No. I didn't understand. I just didn't want to see Matt and Brett break themselves the way my parents did. You were right. I couldn't have saved them. But with the money from the oil, I know the ranch will be secure, and they'll be able to take the time to enjoy life more. I always knew Mama and Daddy were happy. That's what I didn't understand. They worked so hard, but they never complained. I guess it was because they loved what they were doing, and they loved each other. Like we love each other.''

"You don't have to worry. The Triple B's going to be a success. But it wouldn't matter as long as you're with me.''

Whispering, "I love you," he touched his lips to hers, then claimed them. The kiss lasted a lifetime; it lasted only seconds. When he raised his head from hers, his eyes burning with a passion that matched her own, his sigh feathered her cheek.

Bending over, she picked up the magazine she'd dropped earlier. "Listen to this, Chace. I have a plan that will make the Triple B the most popular working dude ranch in the country.''

"A plan? One of *your* plans?''

She kissed the frown lines between his eyes. "It's a good plan, Chace. I promise. What the Triple B needs is good advertising. You have everything you need here, and a very good riding instructor—''

"Who can teach our kids to ride. And their kids' kids. As long as we're together, you can plan and do anything you want.''

When he stole her lips for another kiss, the plan took on the strength of the arms that held her. The Triple B would be a force to be reckoned with, and so would their love.

* * * * *

**Separated at birth,
reunited by a mysterious bequest,
these triplet sisters discover
a legacy of love!**

THE WEDDING LEGACY

A brand-new series coming to
Silhouette Romance from heartwarming author

CARA COLTER

Available July 2001:
HUSBAND BY INHERITANCE (SR #1532)

Available August 2001:
THE HEIRESS TAKES A HUSBAND (SR #1538)

Available September 2001:
WED BY A WILL (SR #1544)

Available at your favorite retail outlet.

Silhouette®
Where love comes alive™

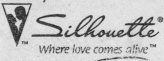

SILHOUETTE®
MAKES YOU
A STAR!

Feel like a star with Silhouette.

We will fly you and a guest to New York City for an
exciting weekend stay at a glamorous 5-star hotel.
Experience a refreshing day at one of New York's
trendiest spas and have your photo taken by a
professional. Plus, receive $1,000 U.S. spending money!

Flowers...long walks...dinner for two...
how does Silhouette Books
make romance come alive for you?

Send us a script, with 500 words or less, along with visuals (only drawings,
magazine cutouts or photographs or combination thereof). Show us how
Silhouette Makes Your Love Come Alive. Be creative and have fun. No
purchase necessary. All entries must be clearly marked with your name,
address and telephone number. All entries will become property of
Silhouette and are not returnable. **Contest closes September 28, 2001.**

Please send your entry to: **Silhouette Makes You a Star!**

In U.S.A.	In Canada
P.O. Box 9069	P.O. Box 637
Buffalo, NY, 14269-9069	Fort Erie, ON, L2A 5X3

Look for contest details on the next page, by visiting www.eHarlequin.com or
request a copy by sending a self-addressed envelope to the applicable address
above. Contest open to Canadian and U.S. residents who are 18 or over.
Void where prohibited.

Silhouette®

Where love comes alive™

Our lucky winner's photo will appear in a Silhouette ad. Join the fun!

SRMYAS1

HARLEQUIN "SILHOUETTE MAKES YOU A STAR!" CONTEST 1308
OFFICIAL RULES
NO PURCHASE NECESSARY TO ENTER

1. To enter, follow directions published in the offer to which you are responding. Contest begins June 1, 2001, and ends on September 28, 2001. Entries must be postmarked by September 28, 2001, and received by October 5, 2001. Enter by hand-printing (or typing) on an 8 ½" x 11" piece of paper your name, address (including zip code), contest number/name and attaching a script containing 500 words or less, along with drawings, photographs or magazine cutouts, or combinations thereof (i.e., collage) on no larger than 9" x 12" piece of paper, describing how the Silhouette books make romance come alive for you. Mail via first-class mail to: Harlequin "Silhouette Makes You a Star!" Contest 1308, (in the U.S.) P.O. Box 9069, Buffalo, NY 14269-9069, (in Canada) P.O. Box 637, Fort Erie, Ontario, Canada L2A 5X3. Limit one entry per person, household or organization.

2. Contests will be judged by a panel of members of the Harlequin editorial, marketing and public relations staff. Fifty percent of criteria will be judged against script and fifty percent will be judged against drawing, photographs and/or magazine cutouts. Judging criteria will be based on the following:

   - Sincerity—25%
   - Originality and Creativity—50%
   - Emotionally Compelling—25%

   In the event of a tie, duplicate prizes will be awarded. Decisions of the judges are final.

3. All entries become the property of Torstar Corp. and may be used for future promotional purposes. Entries will not be returned. No responsibility is assumed for lost, late, illegible, incomplete, inaccurate, nondelivered or misdirected mail.

4. Contest open only to residents of the U.S. (except Puerto Rico) and Canada who are 18 years of age or older, and is void wherever prohibited by law; all applicable laws and regulations apply. Any litigation within the Province of Quebec respecting the conduct or organization of a publicity contest may be submitted to the Régie des alcools, des courses et des jeux for a ruling. Any litigation respecting the awarding of a prize may be submitted to the Régie des alcools, des courses et des jeux only for the purpose of helping the parties reach a settlement. Employees and immediate family members of Torstar Corp. and D. L. Blair, Inc., their affiliates, subsidiaries and all other agencies, entities and persons connected with the use, marketing or conduct of this contest are not eligible to enter. Taxes on prizes are the sole responsibility of the winner. Acceptance of any prize offered constitutes permission to use winner's name, photograph or other likeness for the purposes of advertising, trade and promotion on behalf of Torstar Corp., its affiliates and subsidiaries without further compensation to the winner, unless prohibited by law.

5. Winner will be determined no later than November 30, 2001, and will be notified by mail. Winner will be required to sign and return an Affidavit of Eligibility/Release of Liability/Publicity Release form within 15 days after winner notification. Noncompliance within that time period may result in disqualification and an alternative winner may be selected. All travelers must execute a Release of Liability prior to ticketing and must possess required travel documents (e.g., passport, photo ID) where applicable. Trip must be booked by December 31, 2001, and completed within one year of notification. No substitution of prize permitted by winner. Torstar Corp. and D. L. Blair, Inc., their parents, affiliates and subsidiaries are not responsible for errors in printing of contest, entries and/or game pieces. In the event of printing or other errors that may result in unintended prize values or duplication of prizes, all affected game pieces or entries shall be null and void. **Purchase or acceptance of a product offer does not improve your chances of winning.**

6. Prizes: (1) Grand Prize—A 2-night/3-day trip for two (2) to New York City, including round-trip coach air transportation nearest winner's home and hotel accommodations (double occupancy) at The Plaza Hotel, a glamorous afternoon makeover at a trendy New York spa, $1,000 in U.S. spending money and an opportunity to have a professional photo taken and appear in a Silhouette advertisement (approximate retail value $7,000). (10) Ten Runner-Up Prizes of gift packages (retail value $50 ea.). Prizes consist of only those items listed as part of the prize. Limit one prize per person. Prize is valued in U.S. currency.

7. For the name of the winner (available after December 31, 2001) send a self-addressed, stamped envelope to: Harlequin "Silhouette Makes You a Star!" Contest 1197 Winners, P.O. Box 4200 Blair, NE 68009-4200 or you may access the www.eHarlequin.com Web site through February 28, 2002.

Contest sponsored by Torstar Corp., P.O Box 9042, Buffalo, NY 14269-9042.

SRMYAS2

MAITLAND MATERNITY

You loved
the Maitland
family. Now meet
the long-lost Maitlands...!

In August 2001, Marie Ferrarella introduces
Rafe Maitland, a rugged rancher with a little girl he'd
do anything to keep, including—*gulp!*—get married,
in **THE INHERITANCE**, a specially packaged story!

Look for it near Silhouette and Harlequin's single titles!

**Then meet Rafe's siblings in
Silhouette Romance® in the coming months:**

Myrna Mackenzie continues the story
of the Maitlands with prodigal
daughter Laura Maitland in
September 2001's
A VERY SPECIAL DELIVERY.

October 2001 brings
the conclusion to this
spin-off of the popular
Maitland family series, reuniting
black sheep Luke Maitland with
his family in Stella Bagwell's
THE MISSING MAITLAND.

Available at your favorite retail outlet.

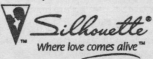

Silhouette®
Where love comes alive™